The Amish Bishop

Samantha Bayarr

Table of Contents

The Amish Bishop

Our Father, who art in Heaven, hallowed be thy name. Thy Kingdom come, Thy will be done; on earth as it is in Heaven. Give us this day our daily bread and forgive us our sins as we forgive those who have sinned against us.

Lead us not into temptation, but deliver us from all that is evil; for Thine is the kingdom, the power and the glory forever. Amen. Matthew 6:9-13

Chapter One

Eva Yoder stared down at the large rocks that bordered the water below as she leaned over the edge of the cutout window just inside the entrance of the covered bridge. Surely, there was a better way out than crashing to her death from the high bridge, but she didn't believe those rocks would hurt long enough to even come close to comparing to the pain that had plagued her since she'd been dating Adam Byler, the Bishop's son.

The outdated wooden structure separated the east side of Peace River from the west and had been condemned several years back after the rotted wood began to crumble under its own weight. The bridge had been an unsafe place to be for many reasons, but this wasn't the first time she'd considered what would happen if she should fall onto the large, white boulders that echoed the moonlight like beacons.

Her breath hitched as she stared down at the large rocks, the choppy water slapping at them as if they challenged her defiance. Her heart raced, fear coursing through her veins like ice water.

From a nest in the rafters of the bridge, an owl hooted, startling her. Her heart rate increased and sweat rolled down the middle of her back despite the early autumn chill in the air. Bile rose in her throat, her fingers gripping the wooden ledge so tightly she could feel splinters piercing her skin.

She would put an end to her pain tonight—one way or the other. He wouldn't let her go easily; nothing about Adam was easy. When they were young, he was different—almost gentle, but the loss of her youth had come painfully fast with every strike of violence against her.

She gazed at the reflection of the full moon off the wind-churned surface of the water and the uneven ripples of light illuminating the dark river. Frogs splashed and croaked on the narrow side of the river, while crickets sang their song, hidden among the tall reeds; fireflies alighted on the thick, brown cattails that stood tall and waved in the breeze. Some folks might consider a night like this to be romantic, but she was too miserable to consider anything besides throwing herself to the rocks below.

Tonight, was the night, and she had to be brave and wait for him so she could tell him her decision not to marry him. She should have told him sooner but now her gut drove her to rid herself of his company once and for all.

To the entire community, Adam was her perfect soulmate and the perfect example of a Bishop's son. He was the community's *Golden Boy*. Eva was the only one who'd seen how rough he could be; he'd managed to fool everyone else. She'd expected the handsome wild-boy would calm down once they were married, but that didn't seem likely since he'd only gotten worse during their engagement; he'd pushed her further than the respectable limit.

Why had she agreed to meet him? Tonight would be no different than any other time. He'd give her a few minutes to enjoy the pleasant, late August evening and the full moon before he coerced her into the dark shadows of the covered bridge where he'd test his limits by putting his hand up her dress. She'd always resist him and he'd slap her playfully at first, until his temper flared and she'd end up in a heap on the damp floor of the bridge.

She had to put a stop to it.

Tonight.

Not just for the sake of her nerves, but for the sake of her virtue.

Each time, he'd pushed a little further, pressing himself against her, trying to entice her into sinful actions with him as if he wasn't able to control himself, and wouldn't wait until they were wed. It was not easy resisting his charms, but the more he pushed her, the more convinced she became that he was not the one for her. They'd been the community's example to the youth as the perfect couple. Having grown up together, Eva was thoroughly aware of his mean streak, but as he grew more handsome over the years, she wanted so much for him to develop an inner beauty, but he hadn't. It seemed the more beautiful he became on the outside, the uglier and darker his inner self became.

Gentle was not a word she used to describe Adam and neither was patient or mature or a whole slew of other virtuous words. He lacked most qualities the other youth possessed, but she was Adam's girl from too many years back to count. Even if she wanted to date someone else, none of the boys would challenge Adam for a chance to date her. He'd made it clear to the other boys from the beginning that she was *his property,* and he'd used his fists to prove it more than once.

Eva rolled her shoulders and rocked her head from side-to-side trying to ease the pain between her shoulders that shot up to the base of her head where it pounded worse than any headache she'd ever experienced. She took in a deep breath and wrung her hands to keep them from shaking. The time to tell him was now, before she lost her nerve. He didn't love her; he loved the feeling he *owned* her—like a plow horse.

He'd broken her ribs during a fight a few weeks ago and she should have had the courage to tell Emily or someone the truth, but lies had seeped from her throat that day, just like all the other times. She covered for him and made excuses for his behavior. In some ways, she'd enabled him to continue to hurt her.

The community, including her own mother, joked about how clumsy she was because of her constant bruises, and she wasn't about to suffer through a lifetime of the same treatment with Adam. She'd seen similar bruises on his mother, and often wanted to go to the woman and ask her about them, but she didn't have the nerve to speak up. On the chance she was wrong, she would insult the woman, and likely be shunned for making such accusations about the Bishop or his son.

The familiar clip-clop of horse's hooves echoed in the night. Her breath hitched; there was no turning back now. He was late meeting her at their *usual spot* that separated his family's home from her mother's. Thoughts of her mother's sadness over the loss of her soulmate entered her mind; she could never have the same kind of love with Adam as her mother had with her father.

His buggy approached slowly. He didn't race toward her; no, he taunted her with the slow trot of his horse as he weaved lazily down the lane toward her. Marrying Adam would certainly benefit her widowed mother in the community; it would assure she was well-provided for once she left home to live with Adam.

Could she let her mother down so easily? The woman had suffered so much already since the death of her husband. Guilt plagued Eva about her decision to reject Adam's proposal, but her ribs still ached from the blows he'd delivered when she'd pushed away his advances the last time. Once the news of her broken engagement would reach the gossipy community, her mother would be looked upon as a failure with her daughter, and she'd suffer a fate almost as bad as being shunned.

Gott, forgive me for shaming mei mamm, but I can't marry Adam.

Moonlight reflected off Adam's perfect smile—a smile so charming he could fool anyone—except for Eva. She knew the truth behind that wild smile of his, and she would not allow herself to fall prey to it tonight. She would fight her physical attraction for him and remember what kind of man he was on the inside. Her *dat* used to tell her before he passed away that some people should be forced to wear their skin inside-out, and Adam was one of those people.

He hopped down from his buggy and rushed to her, pulling her into his arms. She winced from the pain of her still-weakened ribs, but he wouldn't let up on his grip on her. She tried to push him gently, so as not to make him angry, but he was too strong for her.

"Let me go; you're hurting me!"

"You know you like it," he said through gritted teeth.

At six feet tall, Adam was a pillar over her. At barely five feet tall, Eva was fully aware that he could easily overpower her, and that scared her. It was too late to rethink her foolish decision to meet him at such a late hour. Truth was, she had too much to do at her mother's farm and there wasn't enough daylight to get it all done; nighttime was her only respite from her responsibilities.

She'd had to take over her father's chores since he'd become ill when she was only twelve. Resting had prolonged his life for almost two years, and by that time, Eva was well-versed in her father's responsibilities on the farm. Her twin sister, Emily, had been better at taking over for their mother in the kitchen and doing household chores. When their father died, a piece of their mother had gone to the grave with him. She'd become a shell of a woman, and could not get along without the help of her daughters.

Poor Emily was likely to become a spinster, and had planned to take care of their mother for the rest of her days on this earth once Eva got married; she hadn't exactly inherited their father's handsome features. They weren't identical twins, but they were just as close as two sisters could be. Emily would certainly benefit from Eva's decision not to marry Adam. The burden of the farm would no longer fall on her shoulders alone, and they would take care of their frail mother until she went to meet their father in the afterlife.

Adam pulled her closer, kissing her neck, her ribs pinching sharply against the clutches of his arms tightly wound around her waist.

She let out a sharp cry under the vigor of his embrace. "Please, Adam, my ribs still hurt from when you…"

He stopped kissing her and drew his face close to hers, his gaze boring a hole right through her. She shivered, but not from the chill in the autumn air.

"When I what?" he asked, his fiery eyes taking on a mean glint.

She averted his gaze, casting her eyes downward. "Nothing," she whispered.

"Maybe you shouldn't be so clumsy," he said with a chuckle.

"I'm not clumsy," she blurted out, regretting the words the moment she lifted her gaze to meet his angry eyes.

He let go of her and swung his arm, backhanding her in the face so hard she fell back against the railing. She caught herself from teetering over to the rocks below, her heart pounding like a thousand horses' hooves. It was at that moment, when death stared her in the face, that reality hit her. She did not want to fall to her death; she merely wanted to be away from Adam enough to wonder if that was the *only* way out.

She held her stinging cheek and turned away from him, trying not to cry, but the tears flowed uncontrollably. She swiped at them, biting the inside of her cheek so he wouldn't see her cry.

He closed the space between them. "Now, see what you made me do? Why do you insist on angering me? You're my Eve, like in the

Garden of Eden, but you always insist on ruining the mood for me. All I wanted to do was spend a pleasant evening with *mei* betrothed."

"I don't want to marry you, Adam," she whispered, not looking at him. Her heart raced, but it was now or never. She feared death less than she feared this man. Death would be over in an instant, but his violence would stay with her for a lifetime if she married him.

He grabbed her, his jaw clenched.

She stifled her cries; if she resisted him, it would only be worse for her.

He kissed her madly, his hot breath on her neck causing bile to rise in her throat.

"I'll have you, married or not," he said, as he thrust himself against her. "You won't make me wait any longer. I'll have *mei* way, and you'll be *mei fraa* one way or the other."

"*Ach,* please let me go, Adam," she begged through tears.

"Tell me you'll be *mei fraa,*" he said. "If you break our engagement, you'll make a fool of me, and I won't let you do it."

She paused, considering lying to him, but he would see right through her. He would never let her go no matter how much she promised to marry him, and now, she was going to pay for rejecting him. Her knees wobbled and the angry set of his jaw made her quake.

"Please, Adam," she begged around her tears. "All the women in the community in our age group are in love with you." Her voice was whispery and shaky. "You can marry any one of them you want."

He yanked her closer, causing her to cry out from the pain in her ribs.

"I don't want any of them; I want you!" he said, raising his voice so loud, it echoed in the gulch and reverberated across the expanse of the river.

She pushed at him, trying to break free. "I don't want you, Adam."

"I want you to give me what I want or I'll take it!" he said, reaching up her dress.

She wriggled away from him, bending at the waist to keep him from touching her most intimate place, but he ripped at her dress to get to her.

"Let me go," she cried out, yanking her arm to free it from his clenched fist, but he twisted it.

"Please!" she cried out.

He let go of her, surprising her with a blow to her head so forceful it knocked her to the floor of the covered bridge that was too narrow for anything more than foot traffic. She was secluded from the reaches of help from anyone in the span of the many acres that separated her from the nearest farm, including her own. No one would hear her even if she screamed at the top of her lung capacity.

She rolled, trying to get up despite the dizziness and pain that forced her into a stupor.

Adam threw himself on top of her, snaking his hand up her dress.

"No, Adam, please," she cried, trying to wriggle out from under him.

She kicked and squirmed, but he was too strong.

He braced his forearm in her throat to pin her down, cutting off her air just enough that she no longer had the strength to resist him. She gasped for air, but the more she struggled, the more force he used.

I can't breathe; I'm going to die.

She was painfully aware of him ripping her clothes and pushing at her thighs with his knees—until suddenly, everything went black.

Chapter Two

Eva groaned, her skin damp from the early morning dew that had settled on her. Her lashes fluttered, but she couldn't keep her eyes open. Her left eye was nearly swollen shut and she ached all over. She shifted her leg, trying to move, but a pain deep in her belly caused her to cry out. A burning sensation in her loins made her shake.

Birds chirped, though it was barely twilight. How long had she been lying there unaware? She listened, holding her breath; where was Adam? Pulling in a breath was painful; she coughed, her throat hoarse. Trickles of memories from the night before seeped into her brain one-by-one, sobs overtaking her at the violent images replaying in her head.

She pushed herself up from the ground, a flicker of sunlight making its way over the horizon. Her breath hitched at the sight of her torn underwear wrapped around one ankle.

Oh no! Oh Gott, please no!

She reached with a shaky hand to retrieve them. They were too ripped to pull back on so she wadded them up and stuffed them in her apron pocket. She didn't know what else to do with them.

Rising to her knees, she wobbled dizzily.

"I need to get home," she mumbled, her voice scratchy. "*Mamm* will wonder where I am."

She had morning chores to do. She couldn't let her mother or her sister see her like this; she would have to slip in the back door without them knowing and bathe quickly before

22

she was seen in this condition. Struggling to get to her feet, something trickled down her leg.

She bent her head to look; it was blood.

Her breath hitched as she drew her hand to her mouth to stifle the scream she was sure would carry along the drifting fog in the early morning hour. Her neighbors would be rising from their beds and going out for morning milking or gathering eggs, or feeding their stock. She couldn't chance that someone would hear her. There would be too much to explain; too many questions she didn't know how to answer—not even to herself.

She stumbled along the path that led through the field behind her mother's farm, stopping briefly to wipe away the trickles of blood with the hem of her navy dress and holding it close to her, cognizant of her nakedness. Fear pushed her forward, but she constantly glanced over her shoulder, watching for any sign that Adam was still around.

She stumbled again, her legs weak and shaky. Unable to go any further, she collapsed to the ground. With her face pressed in the dirt, she heaved in a breath and let out a primal scream.

From behind her, a large flock of blackbirds rose from the tops of the dried cornstalks, the fluttering of their wings echoing in the silence of the morning.

Gott, please help me. Something is wrong—very wrong and I don't know what to do.

She hugged herself as she rocked in the dirt and sobbed for several minutes before attempting to get up again. Unable to stand without teetering, she fell back to her knees and began to claw her way through the dirt toward home. Her knees dug into the soil as she neared her farm, stifling her cries when the barn came into view. It was the closest building to her; she could hide there until her sister and mother would leave for the Sunday service. Then she could make her way to the *dawdi haus* where she could clean herself up and hide away from their prying eyes.

Her mother had forbidden her and Emily to enter the tiny cottage after her grandparents passed away the same year her father had left them to go to his grave. Except for a spring cleaning once per year, no one had gone in the place in more than seven years.

She approached the barn with caution, knowing it was light enough that she could be seen from the kitchen window. She looked for it, but didn't see a light in the window of the main house. She crept around the corner, careful not to startle the horses when she entered the barn; if they made even the slightest bit of noise, she'd be found out and she wasn't in the right frame of mind to be talking to anyone.

Slipping through the barn door unnoticed, she made her way past the horse stalls and climbed the ladder slowly until she reached the loft. Thankfully, she kept a few wool blankets up there since she liked to steal away sometimes in the afternoon to read. It was the only place she could get away from the demands of her grownup responsibilities for a few minutes of solace.

Collapsing onto her blankets, Eva closed her eyes and willed herself to sleep. She did not want to think about what happened even for another minute, for fear she would go mad.

The barn door flung open and Eva bolted upright; she'd been in a deep sleep and her heart pounded like thunder from a fast-approaching storm.

"Let's go, boy," Emily said, addressing their gelding.

Eva kept her head down and steadied her breathing, listening to be sure her sister would not find her. What would she do if Emily spotted her? What could she possibly say to her sister that would explain her reasons for hiding? Not to mention the way she must look. Emily would probably accuse her of drinking at a wild *rumspringa* party like their cousin, Alma, did every Saturday night. Then, Eva would have to lie to her to explain more bruises and the dirt on her clothes and her skin.

Still, she longed to be in the safety of her sister's arms wrapped snuggly around her, to have her whisper words of comfort in her ear. She needed to cry and to speak out without judgment but she wasn't certain her sister could do that.

An approaching buggy made Eva lift her head just enough to peek out of the small window overlooking the driveway.

Her chest tightened, her shoulders shuddering as Adam hopped out of the buggy. It wasn't unusual for him to be there; he'd taken her to Sunday service every week since he'd asked her to marry him, and today was the day they were to be announced. But he had a lot of nerve showing up today.

He hopped down, his smile as bright as ever. It put a lump in her throat to think that once upon a time she'd loved him and wanted to marry him. Now, she hated him.

Primal instinct filled her mind with the desire to run screaming from the barn and club him over the head with a log from the wood pile, but her conscience and fear of him kept her paralyzed and hidden from his sight.

He entered the barn and approached Emily.

"Is your *schweschder* ready to go?" he asked. "Today is the big day."

She giggled. "*Jah,* I'm so excited for you both, but I'm afraid I don't know where she is. She hasn't come out of her room yet this morning, but I'm certain she's trying to look her best for the big announcement. She must be a little nervous because she didn't even come down for the morning meal."

"Will you get her for me?" he asked with an impatient tone only Eva was familiar with. "*Mei vadder* wants us to arrive early."

"Do you mind if I ride along with you?" she asked. "*Mei mamm* doesn't know about the announcement and she isn't feeling well enough

28

to attend service this morning. I didn't have the heart to tell her what she'd be missing by staying home."

No! Please tell her no!

"*Jah,* I'd be happy to take you with me," he said in an almost flirtatious way.

Eva bit her bottom lip to keep herself from screaming at her sister to get away from Adam. Surely, he wouldn't hurt her in broad daylight. He'd always acted like the perfect gentleman with her when he'd taken her to Sunday service, and used his best manners during the community meal afterward. Even at working bees, he acted respectable. It was only when they were alone at night that he was full of lust and violence toward her.

Emily handed Adam the harnesses. "Would you put these away while I get her?"

"Please tell her to hurry," his tone dripping with fake politeness.

Emily skipped out of the barn; Eva held her breath, fearing he could hear her heartbeat that pounded in her ears. She listened to the muffled noises as he hung the bridle and bit on the peg.

He patted the horse.

"Looks like you won't be working off any of your barn-fat this morning," he said to the animal.

The horse whinnied his response and stamped his hoof on the barn floor.

Within minutes, Emily entered the barn. "She's not here. It looks like her bed hasn't been slept in," she said, worry in her tone.

"Where is she?" he demanded.

From the loft, Eva flinched. She covered her mouth with the blanket to keep her frightful breathing from being overheard.

"I don't know," Emily said. "Wasn't she with you last night?"

He paused. *"Nee,* she never showed up to meet me."

Liar!

"She might have stayed over with Alma in town."

"She's got no business with that Jezebel," Adam said angrily. "Alma is not a *gut* influence on her. I would hate to think Eva's betrayed me with another *mann.*"

He's putting ideas in Em's head that someone else is to blame for what he did to me!

"*Ach,* she wouldn't do that," Emily said. "I'm sure she was up late, having last-minute girl-talk with Alma and they lost track of time. Our cousin is not as bad as the community gossips about her; she would never get Eva into trouble, and *mei schweschder* is not that kind of girl; shame on you for saying such a thing. I'm sure she'll drop Eva off at your *haus.* You'll see, I'm sure she's already there waiting for you."

What could he say to argue with that? If he did, he would give it away that he had been with her last night, and then his violent act against her would be found out. Eva counted on him to play along. She didn't want her sister going anywhere with him if he was in a bad

31

mood, but she was fairly certain he wouldn't risk being caught in another act of violence. Besides, she needed them both gone so she could retreat to the *dawdi haus* and take a hot bath. She would rather Emily went alone than with Adam, but he was very determined to escort her.

"I hope you're right," he relented. "Let's go."

No, Em, don't go with him!

She wanted to warn her sister, but she could not move; fear paralyzed her. If Adam found her there, he would come after her again and he'd hit her and…

Eva held her breath and listened for them to leave the barn. Raising her head enough to watch him assist her sister into his buggy, screams stuck in her throat, but she could not find her voice.

Gott, please protect Emily.

After Adam's buggy left the driveway, Eva collapsed onto the blankets and sobbed mournfully over the loss of her innocence.

Chapter Three

Eva climbed down the ladder, almost slipping on the rungs, her arms and legs too shaky to hold on. With her mother in the main house, she could not risk being seen. It was unlikely that the woman would get out of bed; Emily had probably served her the morning meal in her room. Still, she had to be careful not to be seen in her condition.

She walked slowly toward the barn door, stumbling twice. Collapsing against the frame of the door, she took a few deep breaths to steady herself. In the corner, she spotted the old rake handle her father was always going to put a new set of tines on but never got around to it. Figuring it would make a good walking stick, she grabbed it, hoping it would steady her while she made her way to the *dawdi haus.*

Bright sunlight assaulted her when she opened the barn door, causing her to shield her swollen eye. Making her way across the yard was not an easy task, even with the use of the rake handle. It sank into the damp ground, making her walk tougher than it would be if she hadn't used it. Without thinking, she dropped it to the ground and continued to shuffle her feet the rest of the way.

Lord help me to make it, please, I don't want to die out here for mei familye to find me in this condition.

Her last step seemed like the worst, but she made it. She opened the door and walked in, collapsing into her grandmother's rocking chair.

Her mind wandered to a happier time in her life, a time when she was content to sit at the woman's feet and ball up yarn so her grandmother could crochet shawls for the women in the community.

Leaning her head against the back of the chair, she rocked gently and allowed herself to sob without worrying that someone would hear her.

She missed her grandparents. She missed her father. She missed her mother's bubbly spirit and the way she used to hum hymns from the *Ausbund* when she'd bake bread. Every time Emily baked bread, the house smelled like bread and yeast, but whenever her mother would bake, it smelled like *home*. Their lives had not been the same since their father's passing. It wouldn't be long before their mother joined him. Would she, too?

Adam had left her for dead; why hadn't God taken her? It would have been easier. Death could call her now and she would not object.

Lord, please give me a reason to live.

She rose from the chair and groaned, her ribs pinching her; it was possible the fractures had cracked again. Shuffling to the bathroom, she held onto the walls for support, letting out a cry every time she leaned in the wrong direction.

In the bathroom, she lowered herself onto the edge of the large garden tub her father had installed to help with his mother's arthritis. She turned on the water, knowing it was still hooked up to their LP gas tank out back. At least a hot bath should help soothe the aches in her body. As for the aching in her heart, she had no idea how to fix that.

With the tub filled, she carefully raised her dress over her head and let it fall to the floor. She stared at herself in the mirror, noting her purple and red eye, the lid so puffy it was half-closed. Bruises covered her arms and ribs. It wasn't until she eased into the water and leaned back that she saw the bruises on her inner thighs. She began to cry all over again, her voice raspy, some from crying so much, and some from Adam choking her.

Lord, I hurt so much; show me what to do. I'm so scared. Give me a reason to live.

Eva pushed up the sleeves of her grandmother's nightgown that she found in the cedar trunk and lit the gas stove with a match. She placed the iron skillet on the flame and cracked four eggs she'd taken from the barn and let them drop into the warmed pan. She'd been grateful Emily hadn't done a full milking so she was able to get some milk from Daisy rather quickly.

She'd been hiding in the *dawdi haus* for three weeks and had finally gotten up enough strength to eat on a fairly regular basis. She'd cried until her head hurt so much the first week she just couldn't cry anymore. Though it was a strange comfort in wearing her grandmother's clothes, she'd managed to swipe a few items off the clothesline each time her sister had done the wash, which had seemed to fall on odd days. She'd been able to get away with taking a few pairs of her underclothing and two dresses off the clothesline so far without Emily noticing. She suspected that with her *missing*, her poor sister had fallen behind in the chores, which would account for washing being done a load every few days instead of the usual once-per-week schedule they'd kept to with the community.

Guilt plagued her for leaving the burden of the farm chores on Emily's shoulders alone, but she still wasn't in any condition to help her—even if she could bring herself to come out of hiding. She couldn't even help herself right now. She'd sleep most of the day to keep from having to think about what had happened to her, hoping each time she would feel better when she woke up, but she didn't.

Eventually, she'd be found out if she tried to stay in the *dawdi haus* too long, so she planned to wait for the right opportunity to go into the main house and pack her things. She would stay with Alma in town because she couldn't stay here any longer. It was only a matter of time before she would run into Adam, and she didn't know if she would ever be able to face him after what happened. One thing was certain; she would never let him get close enough to hurt her again.

Eva stood at her mother's bedside and leaned over to kiss her on the cheek. She'd packed her bag and gotten word to Alma by way of sneaking into the community phone booth at the main road on the other side of their field. Her cousin would be at the end of the road in half an hour to pick her up. She had written Emily a letter explaining everything the best she could without confiding in her what had happened. Even Alma didn't know; she would take the secret with her to the grave.

"I love you, *mamm,*" Eva whispered.

Her mother startled her by grabbing hold of her hand. The room was dark and she had assumed her mother was asleep at this late hour.

"Where are you going?" she asked her daughter with a weak voice.

Eva swallowed the lump in her throat and bit back tears. She hadn't seen her in a month, and it frightened her at how frail the woman sounded. Her heart was breaking and already missing her mother but no matter how much she needed to stay to care for her mother, she couldn't live in the community with Adam there.

"I'm going to visit with cousin, Alma, for a little while," she said.

"How long will you stay?"

She let her gaze drop. "I don't know, *mamm,* but I'll send word to you."

"I love you, *dochder,*" her mother said.

"I love you too, *mamm,*" Eva said, bending to kiss her mother again.

She straightened her spine and bit back tears as she left the room. She didn't intend to see Emily; she would only try to talk her out of leaving, but only because she wouldn't understand. She was certain her sister was plenty angry with her by now, and it was probably best if she remained angry. It would drive her to prove she could handle things without Eva, and she needed all the anger behind her to handle things in her absence. The last thing their mother needed was for both her daughters to fall apart. She would need Emily's strength, something Eva just couldn't give to her right now. She barely had the strength to keep herself alive at the moment, and she had no idea how long it would take her to get rid of the cloud of doom that had settled over her.

Eva crept out into the hall and down the stairs, holding her breath until she slipped out the back door. She stood on the stoop for a minute listening to the crickets, the air was damp. It was only the first week of September, but already the smell of turning leaves hung in the low-lying fog. Winter would soon be upon them, and she prayed that spring would renew her the same way it did the world around her. It would be a long hard winter, and a lonely

Christmas without her mother and sister, but perhaps by then, things would mend themselves.

She was supposed to be getting baptized this Sunday, but her baptismal classes had been for nothing. There would be no baptism and no wedding in her immediate future. By now, the entire community had been told Adam's version of how she ran out on him, but they would never know her reasons behind her decision, nor would they know of the violence he'd committed against her. Her story would never hold up against the word of the Bishop's son, and it would bring shame on her own family.

Headlights at the end of her driveway let her know she needed to hurry. She limped down the driveway, her posture a little hunched. Her ribs and ankle were still sore, but she had no idea what had happened to her ankle, except that she must have unknowingly twisted it when she stumbled through the field the morning after *the incident.*

She opened the door to Alma's beat up old hatchback, the tailpipe rattling so loud she worried it would wake Emily.

"Holy crap!" Alma said. "What happened to your eye?"

The girl sounded more *English* every time she talked to her. Would the same thing happen to her after being gone from the community?

Eva had forgotten her eye was still swollen and had a deep purple and green circle around it.

She winced away from her cousin's hand. "Nothing," she said curtly. "I don't want to talk about it. Can we go before this car wakes up Emily?"

"She doesn't know you're leaving?"

"No. She'd only talk me into staying and I can't stay here right now."

"Why, Eva?" Alma asked. "Did Adam do this to you?"

Eva flashed her cousin a pleading look. "I said I don't want to talk about it. Are you going to take me with you or do I have to walk into town?"

Alma punched the gas, and her engine roared down the road even though she wasn't going very fast.

They rode in silence until they reached the stop sign at the crossing. Alma turned toward her. "I think I want to talk about this; if he hit you he should go to jail. That's assault!"

"I don't want to put him in jail because he would eventually get out and then he'd come after me," she said with a shaky voice.

"I bet I could round up some of the boys to teach him a lesson," Alma said with a chuckle. "Have someone his own size pick on him and see how he likes hitting girls after that!"

"Nee," Eva begged. "I just want to forget it and put it behind me."

"Alright, it's your fight!" she said. "But if it was me, and he hit me like that, I would— well, you're right, I'd probably do the same thing. He'd only get out of jail and hit you worse the next time. Best to just put it behind you and put some distance between you and hope for the best."

"Thank you for understanding," Eva said.

"I don't understand—just so we're clear," Alma said. "But I'll respect your wishes and trust that you know what you're doing."

Truth was, she had no idea what she was doing or if it was right. She feared Adam and worried about him getting revenge that could involve something worse than what he'd already done.

The only thing worse than that would be death.

Chapter Four

Emily dressed quickly, seeing that she'd slept in an extra hour. The sun was about to rise and she was already hours behind in the chores. If Eva didn't show up soon from where ever she was, she would have to use the money from the Mason jar to hire someone to till the soil after she'd picked the last of the season's corn so she could get it canned for winter storage. She could get plenty of help from the ladies in the community to organize a canning bee to help her and her mother put away the rest of the corn, but none of the farmers would have time to till her land and theirs. Her only choice would be to hire outside of the community.

Anger filled her at her sister's selfishness for leaving her at such a crucial time. Surely, if she didn't intend to marry Adam, it wasn't worth disappearing over. She'd felt sorry for him because he'd had to endure the service without his betrothed and then had to accept that her sister wasn't going to marry him. She just didn't understand Eva, turning down such a proposal. Marrying the Bishop's son was an honor, and she'd thrown it in his face after all these years that he'd courted her. Emily certainly wouldn't have turned him down; he's the most handsome of all the men in their youth group, and he was polite too, unlike most of the youth.

What she did was just plain rude, to me and mamm, and to Adam.

Downstairs, Emily quickly spotted the envelope on the kitchen table. She sat in a chair and opened it, two hundred dollars fell out onto the table. She unfolded the letter and read it out loud.

Dear Emily,

I don't expect you to understand, but I've changed my mind about rumspringa. I know I'm almost too old, but I decided I better go before I took the baptism. I broke off my engagement with Adam because we just weren't meant for each other and I don't love him the way I thought I did.

I've enclosed some of my rumspringa money for you to hire someone to plow the fields for you. I expect you can put together a working bee for some of the other things you'll need to do before winter sets in.

I hope to see you for Christmas, but for now, trust that I need to do this for my own reasons.

I love you and mamm. Please let me know how she's doing. I'll be at Alma's if you need to reach me.

Love, Eva

"No, Eva," she said aloud. "I don't understand one bit. I think you're selfish and you have no sense of loyalty to this *familye*. As far as I'm concerned, you're no longer part of this *familye*."

Emily tossed the money and the letter onto the floor and let her head sink to the table so she could have a good cry. She was angrier now than she was a few minutes ago, and if she wasn't careful, she would be tempted to confront her, but that would involve going into town and she had too much responsibility to deal with all on her own right now.

Then an idea sparked in her. She picked up her head and wiped her tears. Adam's father didn't have a large farm; his mother kept a large garden, but there was no land to till, and they had very few animals to tend. Perhaps he would be willing to help her in the weeks to come. She would have to remember to ask him next time she saw him.

Just because Eva wasn't going to marry him didn't mean she had to stop talking to him.

He'd been very kind to her for the past weeks since Eva had run off, and Emily saw no reason to turn her back on his kindness.

Emily flung open the drapes in her mother's room, hoping the sunshine would put a little life back into the woman. She'd stayed in bed all day yesterday, and she hadn't been able to pry her from the room. Ever since Eva disappeared over two months ago, her mother had been acting more depressed than usual, and it was only getting worse.

"It's Saturday, *mamm,* the day of the picnic. Autumn is half over and this will be the last time everyone in the community will gather until the winter wedding season. "Surely, you don't want to miss the picnic."

Truth was, *she* didn't want to miss the picnic, and she didn't want to go with guilt hanging over her head all day if her mother stayed home. For the past couple of months, she'd been so bogged down with every chore on the farm, she was ready for a relaxing day with friends and food she didn't have to prepare. She'd bring along a loaf of bread she'd made the day before and some left-over honey-butter, but she was not about to lift a finger today if she didn't have to—other than hitching up their buggy.

"I think I'd like to stay in today," her mother said with a blank stare on her face.

"Eva isn't coming home," Emily said impatiently. "And lying in this bed isn't going to bring her back any more than it'll bring back *Dat.*"

She sucked in a breath. She was so overtired, crankiness had settled in her along with resentment for Eva. Still, that was no excuse to speak to her mother that way.

She lowered her gaze. "I'm sorry, *mamm.*"

"*Nee,* I've probably had that coming for some time now," her mother said. "I hope you and Eva never have to live through the kind of sadness I've had to endure since your *dat* passed on," she said. "But maybe if I'd realized sooner how much my sadness has been a burden to you and your *schweschder,* she wouldn't have left like she did. She was sad when she came to me that last night she was home; it was a sadness I couldn't figure out until I saw she was mourning over something—the same way I've been since I lost your *Dat.*"

"*Ach,* what do you mean?" Emily asked.

"Try not to be so upset with her, Em, she needed to get away, just as I suspect you might need to as well."

Emily rushed to her mother's bedside and scooped her hand up in hers. "I don't need to leave, *mamm.* Everything I need is right here. I won't leave you, I promise."

"That's a mighty big promise to make from someone so young and full of life," her mother said. "Promise me you'll learn from Eva's mistake in judgment with Adam and find someone to marry so you can settle down and have your own *familye.*"

"Jah, Mamm, I promise."

She would never tell her mother she had
her eye on Adam now that Eva had tossed him
aside, even though she was aware of how
imbalanced they were because of his superior
level of handsome features. She wasn't stupid;
he would never consider a woman as plain as
she was. Still, she could dream about it quietly
in her heart even if it would never come to pass.

"So, you'll go with me to the picnic,
then?"

Her mother smiled weakly; it was the first
genuine smile she'd seen from her in years.

"Jah, I'll go."

Emily was almost giddy, and suddenly,
she was in the mood to bake some cookies.
Surely, Adam would speak to her if she offered
him his favorite. He'd never been able to resist
her cookies.

Emily walked out to the barn to hitch the horse to the family buggy, but an approaching buggy made her turn around. Adam flashed her a smile and her heart skipped a beat. She hadn't seen him much over the past couple of weeks and she was excited to see him. He was so handsome; how could her sister walk away from such a smile?

He waved and she walked back toward the house and waited for him to park his buggy.

He hopped down. "I thought you and your *mamm* might like a ride out to the B&B for the picnic, and I had to ride right by here, so I figured there wasn't any sense in you hitching that buggy of yours all alone when you could just ride with me."

She smiled shyly. "That's very kind of you, Adam, but I'd understand if you didn't feel up to helping us."

"*Ach,* just because your sister is fickle doesn't mean we can't still be *friends,* don't you agree?"

She nodded vigorously. "*Ach,* absolutely. *Danki,* for the offer; I'll get *mamm* and my cookies, and we'll be right out."

He rubbed at his stomach. "Don't tell me you made cookies," he said, winking at her. "You might want to keep them away from me or they won't make it to the picnic."

She giggled. He was so charming. How could her sister be so fickle? Surely, if Adam had asked for *her* hand, she would have never turned him down to go out on *rumspringa.* She wouldn't mind seeing his smile every day.

She rushed into the house, wishing she'd put on her Sunday dress, but perhaps her light blue was more appropriate for the occasion. A day in the sunshine would bring some color to her cheeks, and that always made her look a little more like Eva.

She ran into her mother's room, eager to fetch her and get going. She would be the envy of all the girls in the community if she showed up with Adam, especially since the gossip had already made its way around to everyone that her sister had broken off her engagement with him.

Her mother was dressed and waiting for her on the chair by the window. "Was that Adam I saw pulling into the yard?" she asked.

Emily bit her lip to keep from smiling. "*Jah,* he's offered us a ride to the picnic. It was very kind of him considering what Eva did."

Her mother smiled at her. "You run along and don't keep Adam waiting; you don't need me tagging along. I've changed my mind about going. I think I want to work in the kitchen a little today getting the strawberry jam canned."

"*Mamm,* we can do that tomorrow. Don't you want to visit with your neighbors before we're shut in for the winter?"

"*Nee,* Adam is back to being available, and he came here to take *you* to the picnic, not both of us. He was being polite by inviting me to go along. You'll have more fun without me. You run along, I'll be alright here."

She bent down and kissed her mother's cheek. "Thanks, *Mamm*. I love you."

"I love you, too," she said quietly as she glanced out the window.

"I won't stay long," Emily said.

"You go and have a *gut* day.'

"I will, *Mamm*. Don't work too hard in the kitchen. I'll see you in a couple of hours."

She smiled and left the room; she was almost happy that her mother had changed her mind about going. It would give her a chance to be alone with Adam. Perhaps she could lure him in with her baked goods. Her mother had always told her the way to a man's heart was through his stomach.

Maybe I should bring both batches of cookies along just in case!

After packing the extra cookies in her basket, she took in a deep breath and walked out to Adam's buggy, trying not to be so obviously giddy about the opportunity to be alone with him.

"I'm sorry, but *mei mamm* decided she wanted to take advantage of the sunny day and can the rest of our strawberries into jam for the winter."

He took her arm and assisted her into his buggy. "I have a confession to make; I was hoping she would change her mind so we could go alone. I'd like to talk to you if that's alright with you."

Her heart sped up. Was he going to ask to court her?

Chapter Five

Adam sat close to Emily in the buggy and the excitement of it warmed her cheeks. She glanced at his warm leg that touched hers, noting he had plenty of room on the other side of him that he didn't have to sit so close to her. She had to admit it excited her that perhaps he wanted to sit so close.

He tapped the reins against his gelding and the buggy lurched forward causing her to lose her balance and grab the nearest thing to her—his leg.

She quickly snatched her hand away.

"I'm sorry, I lost my balance a little. I'm not used to riding along—I'm used to doing the driving and having something to hold onto."

"I don't mind," he said with a chuckle. "You're more than welcome to keep your hand on my leg if it makes you feel safer. My horse has a mind of his own and you never know if it might happen again."

Heat rose in Emily's cheeks, her hands twisting in her lap. Surely, he wasn't encouraging improper behavior? What would his father or the elders think of her if they rode up to the picnic with her hand on his leg? They would likely be talking about her in some of the same ways the talk had already circulated about Eva. Her sister's sudden disappearance and broken engagement had some people wondering why, including herself, and she wanted to know who would start such vicious rumors. Not only did those rumors question Eva's morals, they were downright unholy.

"Don't suppose you'd give me a little taste of those cookies," he begged. "I can smell them and the temptation is more than I can handle."

She giggled as she retrieved the basket from behind the seat. Lifting the napkin from the top of the basket, she pulled out a cookie and he turned his open mouth toward her.

She hesitated.

He pursed his lips. "Are You going to leave me salivating over that cookie, or are you going to pop it in my mouth? If I let go of the leads, my horse is liable to run us off the road."

He smiled mischievously. What was he up to? Was he baiting her?

He surprised her by grabbing for the cookie with his mouth, capturing the tips of her fingers softly with his lips. She jerked her hand away and dropped the rest of the cookie on the floor of the buggy.

He shook his head. "I'm so disappointed you wasted that perfectly *gut* cookie."

She wiped her fingers on her dress, feeling a little strange about his forward actions. Perhaps she should have insisted her mother go with them as an escort.

"What did you want to talk to me about?" she asked.

He lifted his chin and smiled. "I don't know; I can't think about anything else besides that scrumptious cookie right now. Maybe if you give me another one, I'll be able to think straight."

She took another one from the basket and set it on his leg, being careful not to touch him, then, she scooted to the side to put the basket away and purposely remained at a distance from him. His forward actions had made her a little uneasy. He'd just separated from her sister less than a few months ago; was this all a brave front, or had he gotten over Eva that quickly?

"I'd like to see how the day goes, and we can talk later," he said with a wink and a smile so bright her heart swelled with an infatuation for him.

She nodded and smiled, her cheeks heating.

As they pulled into the large parking area at the B&B, Emily spotted her friends and waved, making sure they noticed who had driven her to the picnic. Their wide eyes had not gone unnoticed by her or Adam.

"I think we're turning a few heads," he said with a chuckle. "Looks like you're the envy of all the single women."

Her heart sped up and her cheeks heated. She'd never dreamed she would be envied by anyone, but she also never dreamed she'd be attending a community function with the Bishop's son or going for a buggy ride with him, either.

He parked the buggy under a shade tree and went about the chore of unhitching his horse to give him a rest. She took her time gathering her things from the buggy and waited patiently for him to assist her down.

He reached for her hand and her heart thumped an extra beat. Adam tucked her hand in the crook of his elbow, giving the appearance that they were more than just riding companions.

"Aren't you afraid that people will talk?" she whispered.

"They're going to gossip anyway," he said with a smirk. "Might as well give them something *gut.*"

"*Ach,* I'm not certain that's such a *gut* idea; I don't want it reflecting badly on Eva."

He stopped in his tracks, his jaw clenching. "I don't care how it makes your *schweschder* look," he said through gritted teeth. "She made her decision, and now I'm making mine. I don't want to hear another word about her if you don't mind."

She nodded, though his anger bothered her just a little bit. She shouldn't have brought up Eva so soon with him. Surely, he was humiliated after the way her sister handled herself regarding their engagement. She wished she could say she understood, but Eva hadn't given her any explanation, and she was certain she hadn't given Adam one either.

"Will you excuse me for a minute?" Adam asked. "I have to speak to *mei dat* for a minute before we eat."

Emily smiled. "It's alright; I'll put my cookies and things on the dessert table."

"Wait for me there; I'll be right back," he said.

She nodded and they parted company. Emily walked toward the long row of pies, cakes, and cookies set up on a table under the shade of a large oak tree. Priscilla Schrock stepped from behind the tree, startling her.

"Are you the reason Adam and Eva broke up?" Priscilla asked in her normal snotty tone. "Or are you her replacement?"

She didn't want to be her sister's replacement, but even if she was, she would be lucky to get such an offer. The only problem with that, she didn't want Priscilla pointing it out to her.

Priscilla Schrock had been a thorn in Emily's side ever since she came to the community to live with her aunt after her parents passed away. She was so mean, she often imagined her parents must have dropped her off with her aunt and ran off. She understood how mourning for a parent could bring hardship, but she suspected Priscilla was simply born mean.

Emily ignored her and walked past, placing her cookies on the large table with the other desserts.

Priscilla followed her. "*Ach,* I heard your *schweschder* got herself into a little *trouble!*"

She whispered the word, but it was loud enough for Emily to hear it.

She turned to face Prissy, as most of the young women referred to her. "Please mind your own business. My life is none of your concern and neither is Eva's."

Prissy leered at the cookies Emily set down and turned her nose up at them. "I think you should watch eating so many sweets. You're already too homely to find a husband; you don't want to lessen your chances by putting on weight."

Emily bit her lip to keep from saying something she shouldn't.

"I wouldn't imagine Adam brought you here as anything more than a friend," Prissy said. "Why don't you save yourself some embarrassment and get a ride home from someone; I'm going to ask Adam to take *me* home from the picnic."

From out of nowhere, Adam was suddenly at her side with his hand on the small of her back. She was so aware of him and the heat that consumed her from his touch, it caused her to have tunnel vision.

"I brought Emily here as my *date,* Prissy, so you can go home with whoever you came here with," Adam said with more politeness in his tone than she would have used.

He whisked her away from the trouble-maker and guided her down toward Goose Pond, which sat on the edge of the B&B property. He tucked her hand in his as they walked, and she worried about what was being said behind their backs. Surely, the entire community was watching them walking to a secluded spot at the edge of the pond.

"I'm sorry if I overstepped my boundaries a little back there," he said. "But if Priscilla Schrock thought even for a minute that I was truly single, she'd have me married to her by the end of the week."

Emily sighed; was he using her?

"That probably came out all wrong," he said. "What I meant was to thank you for allowing me to escort you, and I'd like to ask if I can court you."

Emily stared at him and paused. Was he really interested in her, or was she a cushion to keep others—like Priscilla, from trapping him into a marriage he didn't want to be in?

"I meant—after a respectable amount of time has passed; then it would be proper for me to begin courting again," he said.

Emily's heart sped up and she wrung her hands. If he was really interested in her and wanted to court her, how long would they wait? Until more time had passed—possibly after Christmas? Had enough time passed already that he should be so eager to move on?

"Perhaps after a little more time has passed," she said, not wanting to sound as eager as he was. "It would be acceptable—and even nice if you would begin to court me, but I'd like to get Eva's blessing."

He glared at her furiously, and then grabbed her arms, giving her a little shake. She let out a strangled cry and he immediately righted himself.

He pulled her into a hug. "I'm so sorry," he said. "Please forgive my temper; I'm so hurt by what your *schweschder* did, I just wasn't thinking straight. I didn't mean to frighten you."

"I'm alright," she lied. She was shaking, and she wanted to believe he was merely grieving the loss of Eva. They'd been as close as two people could be during their growing up years, and had been deeply in love—or so it seemed—up until a few months ago. Perhaps it was better if they put a hold on any plans to court until Emily was certain he was over her, and Eva would not return to him for the same reason.

They rode home from the picnic in silence, except for an occasional mention of the weather or activities at the picnic they randomly recapped. She supposed he made small talk with her to fill the awkward silence between them, but Emily had barely noticed. Her mind had been preoccupied with wondering if he would try to kiss her before he dropped her off.

Unsure of how she would react to such an advance, she replayed the scene in her head as if it had already happened. She was nearly overcome with a bad case of infatuation by the time he pulled his buggy into her driveway.

He assisted her down from his buggy, drawing her close to him, and she panicked.

"Would you like to come in and say hello to *mei mamm?*" she blurted out.

He nodded. "I'll step in for a minute—just to keep things *proper.*"

"*Danki,*" she said, putting the key into the lock.

Smoke assaulted them as she pushed the door open; from the smell and the crackling sound, something was burning and bubbling on the stove.

The smoke was so thick, they couldn't see into the room. "You wait here and I'll see if I can find the source of the smoke; do you have a fire extinguisher?"

"Right inside the door," she answered.

He ran into the house but the smoke was too thick. She held open the screen door while Adam fanned the smoke with the back door. As the smoke began to clear, Emily spotted her mother lying on the kitchen floor in a heap. She rushed to her side and collapsed onto the floor beside her.

"*Mamm,*" she cried. "Are you hurt?"

The woman didn't respond. Adam sank to the floor beside her and lowered his ear to her chest, and pressed his fingers to her wrist.

"Adam, go to the payphone and call for an ambulance," Emily cried.

He raised his head and lifted his gaze to meet hers, his fingers still clenching her wrists.

He shook his head. "It's too late for that."

Chapter Six

Eva hung her head over the toilet and emptied her breakfast. A cold sweat coated her skin as she lowered her aching head down on the bathroom rug. For the past week solid, she'd not been able to keep much food in her stomach. She hadn't been sleeping, and she'd become somewhat of a shut-in. Alma had tried her best to pry her from her apartment, but her efforts had been in vain. Eva had no desire to go anywhere and no strength even if she did want to. Had she developed the same illness her mother had been stricken with after their father had died?

The woman had been so sickly and frail she'd spent days in bed. Would she become frail because of her depression too? The only thing is, she didn't ever remember her mother being this physically ill from her depression.

Alma knocked on the bathroom door. "Are you sick, again?" she asked through the closed door.

Eva groaned her answer as she laid her head down on the cold tile and grabbed a towel that hung over the edge of the tub, and tucked it under her face.

Alma knocked again. "Do you need some help?"

Tears dripped onto the floor, her lower lip quivering. She needed help getting up and getting back to her bed, but she didn't want her cousin to see her like this. It would only make her more insistent that she get outside and get a little sun before winter struck them with the first snow of the season. She didn't want to face anyone; shame had filled her to the brim and her spirit was utterly crushed. No matter how many baths she'd had since Adam had violated her, she just didn't feel clean enough. Her bruises had nearly disappeared, but her body still ached and her spirit remained broken. She lay there staring at the honeycomb tiles on the floor, unable to move without convulsing with dry heaves.

Oh, Gott, please help me.

The bathroom door creaked open, and Alma knelt beside her, smoothing her hair. She put the back of her hand to Eva's forehead, moving to her neck.

"You don't have a fever," she said. "But you've been sick for more than a week; maybe it's time we went to the doctor."

"*Nee!*" Eva blurted out. "I'm fine; I don't want to see a doctor."

Her heart thumped. Would a doctor be able to tell what happened to her after an exam?

If she told anyone the truth, Adam might come after her again. So far, he'd left her alone, even though she was certain he knew where she was. She didn't plan on returning to the community; Emily and her mother would have to come to her if they wanted to see her because she had no desire to run into Adam.

Eva lifted her head and hung it over the commode once more, dry heaves clenching her gut so hard she nearly lost her breath.

Alma handed her a wet washcloth to mop up her face, and then sat on the edge of the clawfoot tub.

"Eva," she said, clearing her throat. "Is there any reason to believe you could be—um—pregnant?"

The very word brought bile back in her throat. Tears stung her eyes, and she choked out the rest of the contents of her stomach around the lump in her throat.

Sobs burst from Eva from deep within her gut. It had already entered her mind, but she'd pushed it back and tried to ignore the possibility. The signs were there and she couldn't deny them; she'd seen them in women in the community and it was something she often overheard them discussing during quilting bees.

Alma lifted Eva's quivering chin, forcing her to look at her. "Oh, Eva, you didn't…"

"Nee," she sobbed. "I didn't *let* him; I told him no. I begged him to stop, but then I passed out after he hit me again. When I woke up…I can't even say it because it's too horrible of a thing to say out loud."

Alma pulled Eva into her arms and rocked her trembling frame lightly. "Do you think he *forced* himself on you?"

Eva nodded, fresh sobs bursting from her throat. *"Ach,* I've tried to put it out of my head, but I see him in my dreams…I can't make it go away no matter how much I try."

Alma smoothed Eva's blonde hair away from her face. "If I'd thought for a minute this was anything more than him slapping you in the face, I would have insisted you go to the hospital, but I would have never believed Adam was capable of hitting you, much less forcing himself on you."

"I'm so scared," Eva sobbed, her shoulders shaking uncontrollably.

"I know you are, Eva, but we have to find out for sure," Alma said. "Let's not freak out until we know for sure and for certain."

"I can't go to the doctor; they'll ask too many questions."

"We don't have to," she assured Eva. "We'll get one of those home-tests from the pharmacy. We'll check and then figure out what you want to do—depending on how it turns out."

"*Nee,* I don't want to know."

"Eva, you have to face this sooner or later, and you're eventually going to have to tell the truth to someone other than me. Adam has committed a crime against you, and you must make him accountable before he hurts someone else."

She didn't believe he would hurt anyone else; he'd only hurt her because he could never have her, and he wanted her to be his alone. All the other young women in the community would throw themselves at him now that he was available, but he would reject all of them. He didn't want any of them—only her.

"I won't marry him if I'm pregnant," she said. "I won't give him another chance to hurt me, and that's what would happen if he found out about it. He would use a child to keep me tethered to him like an animal. I'd rather be shunned than to marry him."

"What about making him responsible for what he did to you?" Alma asked. "Don't you think he should be held accountable by the law?"

Eva couldn't imagine facing him in a courtroom and having to prove her innocence. She had *English* friends and she'd learned things about the outside world and how difficult such a crime was to bring a conviction. She may have been sheltered and somewhat naïve, but she wasn't oblivious to the workings of the world around her. She certainly understood that what he did was wrong, but she wanted to put it behind her and let it go.

"*Nee,* it's over, and I'd like it to stay that way. I can't go through that in front of him, or having people know what happened to me."

Alma lifted Eva's chin again, forcing her to look at her. "You do know that what happened is not your fault, don't you?"

"I shouldn't have met him so late in a secluded spot," Eva said. "I've been on the receiving end of his bad temper too many times, but I never thought that he'd…"

She began to sob all over again.

"Eva, it's important that you understand you didn't ask him to commit a crime against you. A woman should be able to feel safe in this world—especially with someone she's known all her life. But sadly, we don't really have a way of knowing what another person is capable of until they let us down. It's even harder when it's someone we love."

"I didn't love him like a woman willing to marry him, but I let it go on this long with him because I'm not getting any younger, and I didn't want to end up a spinster like poor Emily will probably be. I stayed with him because he was familiar. I thought his temper would calm after we were married and he could have what he constantly begged me for."

"Instead, he took it from you, Eva!" Alma said through gritted teeth. "He needs to be held accountable for that."

"You know the Amish way is to forgive," Eva said. "It might take me the rest of my life, but I must forgive him."

"Forgiveness is good for your soul, but if you don't stop him, he might hurt someone else."

"I put a stop to it by leaving the community; he won't follow me here, and he doesn't want anyone else. He's spent his whole youth chasing after me and I would never give him an answer to his proposal. I think that made him mad and he lost control."

Alma sighed as she rose from the floor, and then lent a hand to Eva to help her up. "It sounds to me like you're making excuses for him and making it your fault. It isn't in any way your fault."

Eva stood with wobbly legs. "Why does it feel like it's my fault?"

"How could it be? You had no way of knowing what he was capable of until it was too late. Do you want me to go to the store and get you one of those home tests? We might as well find out what we're dealing with."

Eva nodded and went back to her room, collapsing onto the bed and sobbing. Hearing that Alma suspected the same thing she did, caused her to shake, and a cold sweat coated to her skin.

What *would* she do if the test came up positive? Would she keep a child that was forced upon her? Could she have the courage to let someone else raise it as their own? A child needed two parents, didn't it? Would she be able to love a child that was forced on her?

Lord, I'm terrified, but I put my trust in you to give me a clear vision of what to do. I want to do the right thing, even though the right thing was not done to me. Please give me the strength to forgive Adam, and if he should be held accountable, let it be your judgment and not my own. Danki, Lord, for all your many blessings; help me to remember them even in times of trouble. I put my trust in you.

Her eyes were heavy and she gave in to sleep; it helped to make the pain go away.

Alma handed Eva the pregnancy test, offering her a hopeful smile. "No matter what happens, I'll be here to support whatever decision you make."

She took the box and went into the bathroom, locking the door behind her. It wasn't that she intended to keep Alma from knowing the outcome, she simply needed privacy and time to process the results.

After reading the directions thoroughly, she followed them to the letter and then paced the length of the bathroom waiting for Alma to tell her the time was up.

Lord, please don't let the outcome of this test ruin my life or the life of an innocent boppli. Please...give me a reason to live.

"Time," Alma called from outside the door.

Her gaze dropped to the blue and white test in front of her resting on the countertop. Her breath caught in her throat at the sight of the word *pregnant* that appeared on the small digital screen.

She clamped her hand over her mouth to muffle her sobs, but she could hear Alma knocking lightly on the door.

"I'm here if you need me," she said through the door. "Remember, God is in control."

Gott, I asked you for a reason to live; surely, this is not your answer!

How would she face the community, or her own mother now? Adam had shamed her in more ways than she could count, but now there would be evidence of that shame, and it was hers alone. No one would know he had anything to do with the pregnancy unless he admitted to it, and she didn't see that happening. Besides, she didn't want him to know; he might cause trouble for her or the child.

Lord, give me the strength to protect this wee one.

Chapter Seven

Eva cowered behind a large oak tree, her teeth chattering. The winter wind blew right through her, a cold sweat making her shiver. She peeked out from around the tree, watching for them to leave; she wept quietly while she waited.

Emily stood at her mother's graveside, a blank stare in her eyes. The funeral had ended nearly an hour ago but she hadn't moved, Adam clinging to her side. If not for him, Eva would have gone to her sister and grieved with her, but she couldn't let Adam see her.

She didn't think about the possibility of Adam attending her mother's funeral, but she supposed he had to keep up appearances. After all, he was the Bishop's son; how would it look if the Bishop's family was not in attendance of such a loyal member of the community as her mother was?

Adam hovered close to her sister—almost as if to guard her—but from what?

From Eva?

She wanted to pull her sister into her arms and grieve over their mother together, but she couldn't even approach her because of Adam. She'd tried, but fear of him paralyzed her.

She couldn't allow Adam to see her. What was he even doing at her mother's funeral?

She pulled her black wool coat around her and pushed the collar up to keep her damp cheeks warm. How long would she have to wait for them to depart the grave so she could pray for her mother and beg her forgiveness for not being there when she'd passed on? Emily had gotten word to her through Alma, but Eva had been too sick to come to the phone.

She swallowed the bile that threatened to come up as she stood there and shook. How would she ever explain her problems to Emily so she'd understand and forgive her for not returning to the community? She would have to hide her shame until spring when she could hand over her child to strangers to raise as their own. Her heart ached for the child that grew within her; she would never get the chance to tell the child she didn't give it up for selfish reasons. She was soiled and would never have another chance to have a child or a husband; no man in the community would have her now. Her life was ruined, but the child deserved a better life, one that she was not capable of giving.

Emily finally lifted her gaze and Eva tried to duck behind the tree but it was too late; her sister had seen her and walked toward her now.

Eva's knees knocked together, her shoulders stiffened and her throat constricted. Would she be able to keep her composure in her sister's company? She wanted to flee, but her feet wouldn't move. If Adam walked over to her she would run back to Alma's car—if she could move even then. Tears welled up in her eyes as Emily closed the space between them.

"What are you doing over here hiding behind a tree?" Emily barked. "*Mamm's* grave is over there."

She pointed to where Adam still stood. Eva lifted her eyes toward him, making sure he didn't make a move in their direction.

"I'm not going over there as long as Adam is over there," Eva said.

Emily planted her hands on her hips and scowled at her sister. "I can't believe you'd let your breakup with Adam get between you and *Mamm.* She's probably just as ashamed of you as I am."

"I'm sorry, Em, but you don't understand."

"You're right, I don't understand how you can be so selfish," Emily said.

"What do you want from me, Em?" she asked, leaning her weak frame against the tree.

"Are you sick or something?"

Or something...

"I'm fine," she said. "I didn't take the news about *Mamm* very well."

It wasn't the whole truth, but she couldn't let her sister think she was ill; what if Adam put the pieces together the way Alma did? He'd discover she was pregnant with his child and she would never get away from him. The entire community would expect her to marry him or be shunned. Never mind what he did; she would be the one who was blamed. She didn't have the privilege of being the offspring of the Bishop— if she considered being part of that family a privilege.

"I'm going to ask you again; what do you want from me?"

"I want you to come home and end your *rumspringa* because I need help with the farm. I can't do all of it myself."

"I'm not coming back," Eva said. "That's why I left you the money—so you could hire someone to help you. I don't know if I'll ever be back."

Emily clenched her sister's arm. "How can you say that? I need your help."

Eva patted Emily's hand. "I can't help you right now, Em. I need to do what's best for me right now."

And what's best for mei boppli.

"Are you in some sort of trouble?"

That was her cue. It was her opening to tell Emily everything. If she did, it would expose the secret involving Adam and put an end to the animosity between her and her sister. Alma had guessed what happened, but Emily would never guess something that outlandish on her own.

"Why would you ask me such a question?" Eva asked.

"Because Priscilla Schrock made a comment in front of all the youth at the picnic that there's only *one reason* a girl leaves the community the way you did."

"When are you going to learn Priscilla is a bully, and all she knows how to do is put others down and spread lies to make herself look *gut?* She's trying to destroy my reputation so she can be Adam's number one choice now that he and I are through. As far as I'm concerned, she can have him; they are cut from the same cloth—neither of them has a conscience."

"That's a terrible thing to say about Adam, Eva. Just because you don't want him anymore doesn't mean someone else shouldn't date him."

"Anyone who dates him will live to regret it," she grumbled under her breath.

"What did you say?" Emily asked. "I can't hear you with this wind blowing the way it is."

"Nothing; it doesn't matter," she said. "I'd like to visit *Mamm's* grave; will you please tell Adam to leave so I can go over there."

"You're free to go over there with or without Adam; no one is stopping you."

"What business does he have to be at our *mamm's* funeral?"

Emily narrowed her eyes. "In case you forgot, he's our Bishop's son."

How could she forget that?

"And if you must know, he's been very supportive during all this; he was with me when I found *Mamm.*"

"You mean you weren't even there? How could you let her die all alone?" Eva cried.

"You weren't there either," Emily accused. "Don't you judge me; how could I know she would collapse while Adam and I were at the picnic?"

"Adam escorted you to the picnic?" Eva squealed. "Why, Em? Why would you let him escort you?"

"Why should you care? You tossed him aside; he's a free *mann* now, and he can date whoever he wants to—even me!"

The blood drained from Eva's face and a cold sweat washed over her. "*Nee!* Promise me you won't go anywhere with Adam."

"I will promise no such thing," Emily said. "You're acting very jealous for someone who doesn't want him anymore."

"It's not jealousy, Em; you don't understand."

"You're right, I don't understand you anymore; it's almost as if we're no longer twins. I'm my own person now; I will choose who I date. If he asks me, I'd be *narrish* to turn him down the way you did. I'm all alone on that farm now, and I need a husband."

"Em, please don't."

"Why should I listen to you? Are you returning to the community?"

Eva hung her head. "I can't."

"Then you have no say over me. It's probably a *gut* thing *Mamm* isn't here to see what a selfish person you've become. Go tell *Mamm* goodbye; you can tell me goodbye right here and now because I don't care if I ever see you again."

Eva didn't like the defiance she saw in her sister's eyes. If she wasn't careful, she might just push the girl into a foolish decision where Adam was concerned. It was best to wait until the stress of their mother's death had passed before her sister could be reasoned with; she would need that time to muster enough courage to tell Emily the truth.

Eva knelt in the dirt that covered her mother's grave, remembering the way the woman had clenched her hand before she'd left. Had she known then she was going to die? Had Eva's absence broken her heart that much more?

"*Mamm,* forgive me for leaving you when you needed me most. If you understood why I had to go, it would have made things easier for all of us, but I just couldn't bring myself to burden you with *mei* troubles. I wish I could have told you what happened, even though I suspect you know everything now. Please watch over me from Heaven and ask *Gott* to bless me in *mei* time of trouble."

She wept quietly for several minutes until she heard footfalls pushing at the dry leaves that had already fallen from the trees.

Adam approaching her slowly; her breath caught in her throat and nearly choked her. She wobbled to her feet, looking to the left and to the right. Where was Alma? She'd been circling the large cemetery waiting for her to speak her peace over her mother's grave and now, she was nowhere to be found.

"Isn't that touching—crying to your *mudder,* but she can't help you!"

Eva bit her lip; she was too afraid of him to let his comments bait her for an argument.

"Emily tells me you warned her to stay away from me," his voice thundered against the cold October wind that threatened to bring rain.

"Adam, please, leave me alone," she said, her voice shaky. "And leave Emily alone, too."

If not for Alma being close at hand, she'd not have had the guts to speak up, but, where was she? If he hurt her, would Alma get to her in time?

Adam grabbed her arm and squeezed it. "Let's have an understanding, shall we?" he said, gritting his teeth.

Eva let out a strangled cry; her eyes widened at the anger that spread across his face. Her heart pounded, her ears perked, listening for Alma's approaching car but it didn't come.

He gave her a shake. "You're not the boss of me; if anyone should be told what to do, here, it's you. Do we understand each other?"

She didn't answer, her heart pounding in her ears.

He grabbed her jaw, squeezing her cheeks. "Do you understand?" he repeated himself.

She nodded as best she could, his hand still clenching her face.

"Did you tell anyone about our meeting at the bridge?"

She tried to shake her head, but his grip on her was too tight. *"Nee."*

He shook her again—an evil gleam in his eyes. "I know you don't want the community knowing that you're soiled, do you?"

"You soiled me," she whispered, her gaze cast to the ground.

He let go of her long enough to slap her in the face and then grabbed her again. "You have loose morals; I didn't touch you. If you tell anyone that, I'll hurt Emily, and I know you don't want your innocent, homely, twin to suffer for your lies, do you?"

She shook her head, her eyes bulging at the anger in his stare.

"You better keep your mouth shut and don't even think of telling lies about me, or I'll have a meeting with Emily at the covered bridge. Do we have an understanding?"

She nodded, bile threatening to come up her throat; she couldn't imagine her sister having to endure what she had with Adam. She would rather die than to know he hurt Emily the same way because of her. Still, she had to warn Emily—somehow. That wouldn't be an easy task since her sister wanted nothing to do with her. She'd never believe the truth. Her hands were tied.

He shook her once more and left the gravesite. Eva clamped her hand over her mouth to keep him from hearing the cries

Lord, show me the way I can get through to Emily. Protect her and give her wisdom to see danger before it happens. Open her eyes to see Adam for the evil mann he is.

The rumble of Alma's muffler startled her, and she ran to the car as if death itself was chasing after her.

She opened the car door, the look on Alma's face reflecting her ragged emotions.

"I'm sorry I took so long, I got stuck behind all the buggies leaving the cemetery."

Eva jumped into the car and slammed the door. "Go!" she cried. "Let's get out of here."

Chapter Eight

"What happened?" Alma asked as she punched the gas. "Did you run into Adam?"

Eva turned her head away and stared out the window. "I don't want to talk about it," she cried. "It's over and I never have to see him again."

"He didn't hurt you, did he?"

"He can't hurt me any more than he already has," she said, sobbing. "But that's not what I'm worried about."

"Did he guess about the *boppli?*"

"Nee," she said, relieved her slip up went unnoticed. "But I have to keep him from finding out."

She had to convince Alma to keep quiet about the pregnancy, or it could have catastrophic consequences for her sister.

"I saw him with Emily; how are you going to keep him away from her?" Alma asked.

"By making sure no one finds out what he did to me—especially not Emily. He said if I told her or anyone he'd take her out to the covered bridge and…" she clamped a hand over her mouth to keep from saying the words so evil they were unspeakable.

Alma stopped the car suddenly, sending Eva lurching forward. She braced her hand on the dashboard, thankful they weren't going very fast in her cousin's broken-down car.

"Sorry—I didn't mean to stop so fast, but I have to know—did Adam threaten you? He did, didn't he?" Alma asked as she forced Eva to look at her. "And judging by the red marks on your face, I'd say he puts his hands on you again."

"Yes, he threatened me—of course, he threatened me; why would he want anyone to know what he did?"

"Don't you see? If you don't do something about this, he's going to hurt someone else—Emily is going to be his first target."

"Not if I keep quiet about it." Eva's jaw clenched and her throat constricted. Anger filled her veins with fire; she'd wanted to hit him back after he'd threatened her sister's safety. She wasn't a violent person, but her natural instinct was to protect her sister—at all cost.

"Is he taking Emily home?"

Eva nodded, sobs choking her.

Alma pulled back onto the road and turned toward the community.

Eva braced herself against the door frame and dashboard as if she could stop the car. "Where are you going?" Her heart was pounding in her ears so loud, she could hear it over the sputtering of the tailpipe.

"If you won't go to the authorities, you need to tell the Bishop," Alma said.

"I can't do that! Turn around; I don't want to talk to him."

"His father will give him such a lashing, and maybe even shun him; he'll be required to make an example of his son."

"That's worse than trying to put him in jail," Eva cried. "He'll go after Em, and then he'll come after me and maybe even *kill* me!"

"Which is why you should take care of this with the proper authorities; but let's take this one step at a time. Let's get him shunned first."

"His *vadder* isn't going to shun him!"

"Maybe not, but you have to stand up to him; look at you—you're shaking and quivering like he's some sort of giant. Get him with the slingshot—go to his *vadder* and tell him everything—bring down the Goliath in your life because that's exactly what Adam is to you!"

"I know you're right," Eva said. "But that doesn't mean I have the strength to make it stop."

"I've learned a thing or two since I've been out on my own—away from the community," Alma said as she turned down the road to the Bishop's small farm. "I've learned that you can't give a bully an edge over you— and trust me—ignoring does not work. You need to stand up to Adam and fight back with everything you've got. He won't keep his promise to you even if you do keep your mouth shut. He's out of control and you've got to stop him."

"Please don't take me to his *haus,*" Eva begged. Her heart pounded against her ribcage and her breathing sped up. She covered her face, sobbing into her hands. "Please don't make me go there and talk to the Bishop. If Adam comes home and sees me he'll beat me up or *worse.*"

"What could be worse than violating you and leaving you pregnant?"

She thought about it for a second; the only thing worse than what he'd done to her would be if were to do the same thing to Emily the way he'd just threatened.

"I'll try," she relented.

Alma reached over and patted her hand and then turned the car into the driveway of the Bishop's house.

Eva shook. "I can't go in there; I can't tell them what happened. I'm too embarrassed."

"What do *you* have to be embarrassed about, Eva? This is Adam's shame—not yours."

She shook her head. "I can't—I just can't."

"You have to try, Eva," she said. "If you don't get anywhere with them then maybe you should consider going to the police."

"*Ach,* you know that's not the Amish way," Eva refuted. "I'm trying to forgive him, but I don't know how."

"I'm sure even God wouldn't find fault with that under the circumstances," Alma said.

"I pray that you're right."

Alma parked the car and turned to Eva. "Do you want me to go with you?"

Eva lowered her gaze and shook her head slowly, tears forming in her throat. "*Nee,*" she whispered. "It's bad enough that I'm going to have to say it out loud; I don't want you to have to hear any details. This is something I have to do alone—for Emily."

"And for yourself and your *boppli,*" Alma said firmly.

Eva let out a strangled cry. "I won't tell them about the wee one; I don't want Adam to try to stop me from doing the right thing and giving it up for adoption."

Alma reached over and squeezed her hand, whispering a prayer for strength.

"Hurry and get this over with before Adam gets back from taking Emily home," Alma said.

The very thought of him taking her sister home made her cringe with worry for her safety.

Eva opened the squeaky door and stepped out onto the gravel driveway, the slightest hint of autumn leaves burning hanging in the air. Colorful leaves blew across her path as she made her way up to the front porch of the white clapboard home. She knocked lightly on the door and the Bishop answered.

She stood there shaking; she wanted to bolt from the porch, but her feet were as heavy as horses.

The Bishop looked at her over the top of his wire-rimmed glasses, his white beard neatly trimmed just below his chin. "Adam is not here," he said coldly.

"I didn't come to see Adam; I would like to talk to you," she said, her voice barely above a whisper.

"I'm glad to see you've come to your senses and decided to confess."

Her heart pounded in her shoes. "I don't have anything to confess," she said, raising her voice a little.

"Adam tells me you broke off your engagement with him so you could run off and have unholy relations with another *mann.*"

"*Nee!*" she cried. "It's not true; Adam— he *hurt* me."

"I think it's *your* immoral behavior that has hurt Adam." He pushed his glasses up on his nose, his jaw was set. Lifting his straw hat from a hook by the door, he set it on his thinning, grey hair and stepped out onto the porch. He folded his arms across his chest and narrowed his eyes at her. "I will not tolerate you speaking such lies about *mei* son. You'll confess your immoral sins or you will be shunned."

"What about Adam's immoral sins?" she cried. "He *forced* his affections on me."

The man lifted his chin, his jaw clenched. "He is a *mann,* and he has needs; you've teased him for too many years. You should have married him so he didn't have to wait on you. If there is sin between you and Adam, it's your fault. I won't allow *mei* son to marry a woman with such loose morals."

Eva heaved in a breath as if she'd had the wind knocked out of her. "You can't mean that," she cried. "Adam threatened to hurt *mei schweschder,* Emily, if I told anyone what he did to me."

He grabbed Eva by the arms and gave her a shake. She let out a strangled cry, her heart pounding hard enough to burst from her ribcage.

"You keep your filthy lies about Adam to yourself," he threatened. "I'm placing you under the ban; leave my property and the community at once or your *schweschder* will also be shunned."

Eva bit her bottom lip to keep from screaming out to him about the baby; it was her only proof of what he'd done, but he would find a way to disprove even that, and she couldn't chance that Adam would hurt the child if he discovered it was his.

She broke free from his grasp and ran from the porch. Out of breath, she hopped into Alma's car and slammed the door. "Get me out of here," she cried.

"What happened?" Alma asked as she started her car.

"I've been shunned!"

Chapter Nine

"What am I going to do now?" Eva cried as she slumped onto Alma's sofa. "Adam is sure to come after me now that I've told his *vadder* what he did."

"I can't believe he would defend Adam like that," Alma complained. "I think the best thing for you to do is disappear altogether—unless you're ready to go to the police now."

"He accused me of teasing Adam and then being loose enough to give in to him; he'll back up his son to the police and they'll believe the word of a Bishop before mine."

"You could be right," Alma agreed. "Which means we have to hide you so he can't find you; pack your things quickly."

"Where do you think I'm going to be able to go with less than two dollars in my pocket?" Eva asked.

"I have a friend who lives in the Pigeon Hollow community and her neighbor was recently widowed and left with an infant. His aging mother is too old to help him care for the child and he's looking for a nanny. It's a live-in position, and I know I can get my friend to put in a good word for you. You can stay there during your pregnancy and then after the adoption you can come back here or go to a new community. That will give you enough time to sort things out and Adam would never find you there."

Eva began to shake even more. "I don't know how to take care of a *boppli*," she said.

"His mother lives there with him," Alma said. "I'm sure she'd be more than happy to give you instructions. Katie told me the woman has arthritis so bad she can't hold the baby; she could tell you what to do and you could be her hands as if she was doing it herself."

"That seems awfully stressful to have someone standing over my shoulder all the time, especially when I don't know what I'm doing."

"At least while you're there, you'll be able to take advantage of seeing the midwife from their community."

"And when they find out I have no husband," Eva said. "I'll be shunned from that community too."

"No, you won't," Alma said. "Pigeon Hollow is a very little community, and it's about two hours from here, so the chances of you running into Adam there are next to nothing. It would take him more than half a day to get there by buggy."

Eva stopped ringing her hands for a minute and looked at her cousin thoughtfully. "I really appreciate everything you've done for me; I'll get packed at once, but I hope you're right about this. And I hope after all this is over I can go back to my normal life again. I don't know if I'll ever be able to go back to the community because I'll always be afraid of Adam, but perhaps, he'll marry someone else while I'm gone and he'll forget all about me."

"The only person dumb enough and mean enough to marry Adam would be Priscilla Schrock and they are perfect for each other," Alma said.

Eva let out a heavy sigh. "As much as I dislike Prissy, I wouldn't wish Adam on any woman. No woman deserves to be treated like that, not even mean old Prissy."

"I guess I'll have to agree with you there," Alma said. "Let's get moving before Adam has a chance to catch up with us. I'm sure by now the Bishop has told him all about your visit and your conversation with him."

The mere mention of Adam and the possibility she would have to see him again made the blood in her veins run cold. She packed quickly her few belongings, including all of Alma's old dresses that she never wears anymore. She was grateful her cousin had given them to her, but she'd refused the blue dress that was identical to the one she'd worn *that night.*"

She packed quickly and stuffed the two bags in the back seat, then they took off toward Pigeon Hollow.

Eva unpacked her things and placed them in the dresser drawers in the guest room in the Widower Bontrager's house. His mother, who'd been staying at the main house, moved her things back out to the *dawdi haus.* Taking the old woman's place as caretaker of her granddaughter was awkward, but that was the job that she'd been lucky to be hired on for.

There were no surprises there. It was just like Alma said it would be; she'd explained very briefly to the widower that Eva had gotten herself into a little bit of *trouble* and he hadn't even blinked an eye at the news. She'd heard a lot about the community and its lax rules but she never dreamed it would be so easy to fit in here. She was truly grateful for the opportunity to hide away from Adam and make a little money on the side. The only thing that frightened her was that she had no idea how to care for an infant. It was one of the many reasons she'd made the decision to give up her own child for adoption.

She took in a deep breath. "I can do this," she said to herself. "I've held enough wee ones in the community to fake my way through this job. Besides, I don't even think the widower would even notice. Lord, heal that man's heart from losing his *fraa,* and open his heart to receive his *boppli.* Bless me with the hands of a *mamm* to take *gut* care of his *dochder.*"

She took a deep breath and walked out into the living room where the baby was sleeping in a cradle near the warm fireplace. The child's grandmother rocked in the chair beside the infant while she read passages from the Bible that looked nothing like the one the Bishop used during their Sunday services. It struck her as funny that she would read through such a modern Bible but Alma had told her this community was made up of Christians who didn't follow any of the old order ways of the Amish other than the way they dressed. There was even a phone in their modern, electrical kitchen. She could get spoiled with such modern conveniences but ever since the incident, she wanted nothing more to do with old order Amish or their strict ways. None of those rules had protected her that night, and in fact, had protected Adam from punishment from the outside world. Old order Amish had always disciplined their own people and very rarely if ever, involved police in any disciplinary actions within the community. If they did, Eva would feel more confident that Adam would be truly punished for his crimes against her.

She straightened out her apron and reached up to check the pins in her *kapp,* making certain that she was presentable before approaching the old woman. It saddened her that the child's father seemed to be grieving too much to care for the infant on his own. She would do her best to learn quickly, knowing if she failed she would have to return to Alma's house.

Widow Bontrager looked up from her Bible passages when Eva entered the room. The woman nodded to her and held her hand out toward the sofa opposite her. She admired a beautiful crocheted blanket that hung over the back of the sofa and assumed the widower's wife had made it along with the other many intricately crocheted doilies and even the yellow blanket that covered little Grace who slept peacefully in the cradle.

Once she was seated across from the Widow Bontrager, she smiled nervously, forcing herself to put away her own sadness and worries.

The widow smiled back at her. "I'm sorry that you found yourself in a spot of trouble," she offered. "God can save you from your troubles if you let Him."

Eva worked hard to keep her expression from giving away her emotions. She'd not only begged God to deliver her from her troubles, she'd even tried bargaining with Him, but when all was said and done, she was just as pregnant as she was Amish.

"Would you like me to tell you just how easy it is?" the widow asked.

She nodded reluctantly.

The widow smiled and her eyes almost glistened. "It's as easy as taking a little walk with me down the Romans Road."

Chapter Ten

Eva hummed a happy tune while she warmed Grace's bottle. The tightness in her chest was lighter than it had for months—years even. She'd prayed the sinner's prayer with the Widow Bontrager only a week ago, and already, her life had changed. She'd forgiven Adam for the sins he'd committed against her, and had even forgiven herself for the awful thoughts she'd had about him afterward. She still had a lot of healing ahead of her, but she would be ready to move on with her life once the adoption was finalized with her own child.

Taking care of little Grace had filled her with some motherly instincts that were tough to resist—especially since she struggled to accept that adoption was what would be best for both her and the child she carried. She had no way of taking care of an infant without a husband or a stable job. She hadn't discussed with the widow if she would be able to stay on as the nanny after her adoption was finalized. She wasn't certain if she'd have the strength to go back; her heart nearly broke every time she held Grace close, wondering what it would be like to hold her own child.

The midwife had told her that she'd likely go through several stages during her pregnancy, from grief to elation—especially since she'd had to accept that there was no way around having to surrender her child once it was born. She found herself longing to hold her own child, and often found herself cradling her swelling abdomen without thinking. The Widow

Bontrager had asked her on more than one occasion if she'd thought it through enough before setting herself on that decision.

The answer to that question was a very quick *yes*. But the conclusion was always the same; she had no means and no husband in order to care for her child properly. If she wanted to get technical, she was homeless. She couldn't raise a child on the run from its father. The widow had been bold enough to point out that she needed a husband as much as her son needed a wife, but Eva could not let another man get too close to her, and she didn't want a marriage of convenience. Besides, they'd only exchanged glances across the dinner table a few times and had not spoken a word to each other. It was an awkward exchange at best; she couldn't imagine lying next to him in bed or allowing him to kiss her or—or more.

Staring out the kitchen window at the early snowfall, she became temporarily mesmerized by the wispy snowflakes floating and whirling in front of her. they were so light they melted as soon as they hit the ground. Too soon, there would be heavy snow and she would settle in for the winter.

The weeks had passed quickly, and Thanksgiving was in only a few days. She'd longed to visit with Emily over the holidays, but there was no way she could allow her sister to see her in this condition. There was no longer any way to hide the child she carried. There would be no holidays with her sister this year, but at least she would be seeing Alma. If not for her cousin, she'd have probably gone mad from isolation after her first day here.

The Widow was usually good company, though she slept a lot, but her son, the Widower, wasn't exactly friendly with her; he kept to himself and only sat at the dinner table with her because his mother insisted. The two of them hadn't exchanged two words since she'd been there and any questions or concerns she'd had were presented to his mother. Ever since she'd been taking care of Grace, she hadn't seen him hold the child even once since she'd been there.

Would it be that way for her when she gave birth? Would it be better if she never saw the child? She'd thought about it for long hours, trying on every scenario to be sure she'd exhausted all her efforts to make the right decision. In the end, it left her with a lump in her throat and an empty longing in her heart for the child that Adam had cheated her out of being able to hold and care for.

When the bottle was warm enough, she took it back to the bedroom that she shared with baby Grace and noticed her stirring. She'd discovered it was easier if she had the bottle ready on schedule so that she could feed her right away after changing her. She'd gotten used to a schedule with the infant, the routine convenient to keep her mind off her own troubles.

She went about the task of changing her diaper, smiling when she arched her back and stretched. It was difficult to change her when she squirmed like that, but she usually waited a minute before resuming the task.

"You're wiggly this morning," she said with a baby voice. "Are you hungry, my sweet baby?"

The words sounded funny yet natural as she spoke them. She hadn't meant to say it; she was aware Grace wasn't her child, but in some ways, she seemed like she was.

She let out a little cry-yawn and arched her back again. Grace jutted out her lower lip, her face turning red as she filled her diaper.

Eva giggled. "When am I going to learn to wait a minute to change you so you can finish up so I don't have to waste a clean diaper?" she asked with a chuckle. "You'd think I'd know your little tricks by now, my wee one."

She readied another diaper and wet another cloth to clean her up, and then decided instead to run her a bath in the oval, galvanized tub on the bathroom counter. It would make for an easier cleanup and it would give her a chance to work up her appetite so she wouldn't fall asleep midway through her bottle. She'd gotten in the habit of that the past few days and it had caused her to wake earlier than usual. Best to get her sleeping habits established now.

When the water was ready, she put Grace in the warm water and washed her quickly so she wouldn't get a chill. The house was warm enough with the gas heater, but being an old house, it was a bit drafty. She supposed if the Widower Bontrager felt up to putting on the storm windows it would be warmer, but if he didn't take to the chore soon, it would be a drafty winter. It wasn't her place to tell him; perhaps she could mention it to his mother and she could remind him.

The last thing Eva wanted to do was to overstep her boundaries with the man, who'd opened his home to her at a time when she needed it most.

Eva wrapped Grace in a towel and took her back into the bedroom to dress her. The widower had been kind enough to move the cradle into her room to make for an easier night schedule. She began to fuss a little, but Eva knew she would settle down once she was warm and being fed.

"Hold on just another minute while I get your warm nightgown on," she cooed to the child.

Finishing it off with a pair of socks and a knitted cap for her damp hair, she pulled her close and gave her the bottle, walking out to the living room to sit in the rocking chair by the warm fire.

She stopped short of the entrance; the widower stood at the hearth stoking the fire. He turned around and looked at her, aware of her approach.

"I'm sorry," she said, retreating. "I can go back to the room with her."

He looked at her, his kind eyes so inviting, but she'd vowed never to trust another man; her swelling belly was proof enough of that. The only difference was, she didn't fear him the way she feared Adam.

"Nee," he said. "You're welcome to stay; *kume,* get warmed by the fire."

He added another log and the flames brought a golden glow to the room. The wood crackled and hissed; it was a sound that always relaxed her and made her feel at home. Could she ever feel at home here? She glanced over at the widower; he was a handsome man, and only a few years older than she was. Why hadn't she been so lucky to have a man love her so much that his whole world would be in ruins if she should die?

She lowered her gaze and concentrated on feeding his daughter; it was her job and nothing more. No matter how much she wished for such a life with a husband and the chance to raise her child, it was not ever going to come to pass. The sooner she accepted that reality, the better off her life would be. Still, it put a lump in her throat to see first-hand what she'd missed out on by allowing Adam to hurt her.

"You're very *gut* with her," the widower said.

She looked up from the baby, startled by his words. It was the first time he'd spoken to her in the weeks since she'd been here.

"*Danki,*" she said, looking away from him. "She's a *gut boppli;* she's very content."

"I'm very grateful for your help," he said, his tone low and gentle.

"I believe I'm the one who should be grateful," she said.

He nodded, a forced smile tugging at his lips.

She cast her eyes toward the fire to avoid looking into his inviting eyes; his kind words were enough to fool her into getting too comfortable, and it would be too easy to fall for his gentle charms but she was in no position to be giving any thought to such things. Best to put it out of her head before she's tempted to make another foolish mistake. It would do her no good to wish for such a man to care for her when she was carrying another man's child. He could barely take care of his own child and was not in any shape emotionally to care for her, any more than she could do the same for him.

Grace finished her bottle and Eva lifted her onto her shoulder and rose from the rocking chair. "I better get her to bed," she said. "*Danki*, Mr. Bontrager—for everything."

"Please, call me Ben," he said, mesmerizing her with a glimmer in his eyes from the glow of the firelight.

She nodded, casting her eyes to the floor, and then making a fast exit from the room. She rounded the hall to the room she shared with Grace, her heart pounding, her breathing hitched.

Lord, deliver me from wishful thoughts about this haus and the boppli—and especially, the Widower Bontrager. Help me to remember my place here as a nanny to Grace and remove all longing for things that will never be a part of my future. Help me to be content in my circumstances and not want for more than you've blessed me with.

After coaxing a burp from Grace, she kissed her gently on her head, breathing her in. Tears clogged her throat; she loved Grace. How could she give up this wee one when her services as a nanny were no longer needed? How could she give up the security of this home? How could she give up her own child?

Had God given her a reason to live?

She placed Grace in her cradle and sat in the rocker by the window, a hand over her swelling abdomen. Truth was, she loved the child that grew inside her.

Lord, please don't take these things from me if it is your will for me to have them.

Memories filled her of something her mother had said to her when she learned Adam had asked her to marry him. *One day, you will have a boppli of your own—that is when you will learn what true love really is,* she'd said.

"You were right, *Mamm,*" Eva whispered.

Chapter Eleven

Eva stirred when Grace whimpered in her sleep. She shivered as she pulled back the quilt and dropped her feet onto the cold floor to check on the baby and make sure she was warm enough. The wind howled and whistled through the windows; sleet hit the glass with a chorus of *pings*.

Bending down, she lifted the infant out of the cradle she'd outgrown. She'd have to remember to ask the widower—Ben, if he could bring the larger crib into the room. At five months, she'd be crawling any day, and she'd already begun to pull herself up a little.

Eva raised her head and sniffed the air; the aroma of spices reminded her of Thanksgiving at home. She missed Emily and her parents so much it hurt; today was the first holiday she'd ever spent away from her family.

Widow Bontrager had encouraged her to help her bake pies today, but she'd much rather be making a mess of her mother's kitchen and listening to Christmas Carols on the battery-operated radio that her mother kept on the counter. They would sing along to the secular Christmas songs and laugh every time the *Chipmunk's Christmas* song came on.

It was the only time their mother would permit them to listen to *English* music; she kept the radio for weather alerts, but once a year she allowed the indulgence, and it was one of the happiest memories she cherished. And so, began a tradition of listening to the radio while they baked between Thanksgiving and Christmas.

She missed it, and held no hope of hearing it at the Bontrager home—liberal Ordnung or not.

Eva wandered into the kitchen, noting she was too late to help with the food preparation.

"I'm sorry I wasn't any help in the kitchen; Grace doesn't seem to feel well today. She's been very cranky and her temperature is a little high."

The old woman patted her hand and smiled. "You're doing the most important job in this *haus,* and that's taking care of that *boppli.*"

"*Jah,* but I feel like I let you down today," she said. "Is your arthritis any better today?"

The old woman clucked her tongue at her. "Don't you worry about me; you take care of that wee one. I'll bet she's teething."

Eva scoffed. "Already?"

"Sometimes the first tooth can take months to appear, but the fussiness stays on."

"*Ach,* the poor thing; no wonder she's so cranky."

The widow handed her a gingerbread cookie; it was one of her favorites.

"I was able to get the ingredients for your cookies while I was in town yesterday—that is, if you feel up to baking them. You look tired."

Eva yawned; she hadn't meant to. "Grace kept me up quite a bit last night."

"Why don't we wait a few days, then, and you can make them for Christmas season," the widow said. "Didn't you tell me they're more for the winter season?"

She nodded, suppressing another yawn. "They're a Christmas cookie, but *mei mamm* and Emily would make them on Thanksgiving. We listened to Christmas music on the little radio she kept on the table in the kitchen."

The widow raised an eyebrow. "She let you listen to secular music?"

"Only at Christmas time; I missed out on it this year—well, with *mei mamm* gone now." Tears filled her eyes and the lump in her throat could not be swallowed.

The widow clucked her tongue again. "We'll have none of that today; it's Thanksgiving." She went to the cupboards above the refrigerator and pulled out a small radio and plugged it in. "I like to listen to the Christmas music too—especially those chipmunks."

Eva laughed for the first time since she'd left home; it filled her with guilt that Emily would be spending the holiday alone, but Alma had promised to go back to see how she was holding up by herself. Luckily, their father had the sense to provide for them after his life ended. Though it went against the rules the Bishop had laid down, their father had a life insurance policy. It wasn't much, but it would be enough to keep the farm running smoothly without Emily having to get a job away from the family land. The policy had been enough to pay the note on the farm and still afford a little nest egg that Emily could live on for a few years. After that, she would have to start collecting egg money again from nearby farms that don't keep chickens.

The widow cleared her throat. "You seem a million miles away."

"*Nee,*" she said sadly. "Only as far as *mei familye* farm; I was wondering how *mei schweschder* is doing."

"I wish you'd tell her how you're doing," the widow said.

"I could not see her in my condition," Eva said, lowering her gaze.

"You're not showing enough yet for anyone to notice," the widow said, putting a comforting hand on her arm. "Go to her and see her."

"Maybe once I've had the *boppli* and I've recovered from…giving it…to someone…who can take care of it," she said with a shaky voice.

Tears clogged her throat as a warm pair of arms embraced her. She leaned against the widow's shoulder and sobbed for several minutes.

The widow smoothed her hair and shushed her gently. "I get the feeling you don't want to give up the *boppli.*"

"*Ach,* I can't take care of it on my own without a husband or a job. I know that," Eva cried. "But these past few months taking care of Grace has played tricks with my mind and caused me to think too much about something that could never come to pass."

"Perhaps *Gott* will provide a way," the widow said. "There's still plenty of time for a miracle."

Eva nodded and wiped her tears. "Let me help you get the meal on the table while Grace is resting; no telling how long I will have to eat before she fusses again."

The widow lifted her chin and smiled.
"You are a *gut mamm* to that *boppli*—she
couldn't ask for a better *mamm* than you."

With Grace slung over her shoulder and
sleeping peacefully, Eva retreated to the living
room to sit by the fire for a little while. Her
belly was full, but her heart was nearly empty. If
not for the babe in her arms, she'd have felt the
sting of loneliness more than usual today. With
the holiday now behind her, it was time to start
thinking of what she could do to avoid seeing
Emily for Christmas. It wasn't that she didn't
want to see her; she wanted it more than
anything, but if she did, her sister would know
about her pregnancy, and that would require an
explanation she wasn't willing to give.

Ben entered the room and flashed her a
nervous half-smile. "Let me stoke the fire for
you; would you like some hot cocoa or coffee to
warm your insides?"

She looked at him curiously. "Thank you, but I can get some in a minute after I put Grace down."

"I only ask," he said, putting a couple of logs on the fire. "Because I'd like to talk to you about something."

Ach, this is it; he's going to let me go and he's buttering me up with offers for kaffi or cocoa so I won't fall apart after he tells me I have to leave so he can have Christmas with his familye without me in the way. Lord, please soften his heart toward me and don't let him throw me out in the snow.

"I'm fine without it," she said. She had Grace to occupy her hands enough to keep her from wringing them.

"This is a very difficult thing for me to say," he began. "But I think we both have to face reality, and that is—well, we *need* each other."

142

Eva's heart flip-flopped and her breath hitched. Was he about to ask her to stay on even after the holidays?

"What I meant to say…" He cleared his throat and pretended to stoke the fire again even though it didn't need it. "Even though I don't know your circumstances, I know you can't support your own kinner on the salary I pay you after your room and board is taken care of, and it's clear I can't work my farm if I have to take care of Grace all day—well, would you consider a *marriage of convenience* just for the sake of our misfortune?"

Eva sucked in a breath and held it there; she wasn't expecting *that.* "*Ach,* you want to marry me in name only?"

He nodded, his blue eyes full of kindness. "*Jah,*" he said. "I didn't mean it as an insult; I'm only trying to help—both of us. I wasn't expecting to be left with a *boppli* any more than you were, I suspect, and I'm willing to provide for you if you'll take charge of Grace—

permanently. I've seen the way you've taken to her, and she needs the love of a *mudder.*"

Is that what I am? A mudder?

She smiled for the first time in a long time. She could not deny her love for Grace any more than she could deny her growing affections for the child she carried.

"Will you give me some time to think about it?" she asked.

"I will, but I think we should marry before you begin to show much more than you already do; soon, you won't be able to hide it underneath the folds of your dress, or the cover of an apron."

She nodded. He was right about that. He was trying to save her the shame of being pregnant and alone, and she appreciated that, but she'd promised herself she'd never consider another man after what Adam had done to her. Would Ben expect the same thing from her if he was married to her?

She rose from the chair without a word to him. She'd seen a kindness in his eyes that didn't compare to the anger in Adam's, but there had been a time when she'd trusted him, too. Would Ben turn against her the same way Adam had when he didn't get his way?

She shuddered after placing Grace in her cradle, noting that she'd forgotten to ask him about the crib. How could she ask him about it now that this proposal stood between them?

She'd weighed the benefits and risks of marrying in name only—for the convenience of keeping her child and raising Grace as her own. She'd rejected the idea on too many negatives—the main one being that if Adam found out about the child, he could cause trouble for her, the child, and Ben. Getting married had been a dream she'd had for a while, and a loveless marriage did not appeal to her in the least.

Being asked was a whole different story. A proposal made it official—she would be required to think it over and give Ben an answer. It was a lot to consider—almost too much. Would it be selfish of her to keep the true lineage from her child? Since she'd admitted to the Bishop that she'd had physical contact with his son, the entire community would know the child was his.

The Widow Bontrager smiled a gentle smile. "My son wants to rescue you the way he did for Ellen, his *fraa*. Ellen had gotten herself into trouble with an *Englisher* during her *rumspringa*. Her brother, Ebner, is Ben's *gut* friend. He married her to keep her from being shamed in the community. It, too, was only a marriage of convenience."

"I thought all this time he was mourning her," Eva said.

The widow cupped her hand under Eva's chin. "Of course, he's mourning her; he's human, but most of what he feels is guilt because he didn't love her, and now, her *boppli* is a stranger to him."

Eva sighed; it was a relief to know he wasn't just another cold-hearted man. But how would he be with her child if she should marry him? She would have the sole responsibility of caring for two children without the love and care of a husband—only the financial security. Was that enough? She loved Grace already as if she was her own child—how could Ben help but fall in love with her the same way. If only he'd take the time to hold the child or help care for her in any way—the way a real father would. She supposed he couldn't because he wasn't Grace's father and he never would be—just like he wouldn't be to her child. Was it fair for two children to grow up not knowing the love of a father?

Memories of her childhood flooded her mind. Her father had been very much involved in the care of her and Emily. He'd taught them to ride a horse and to plant seeds to make them grow into long rows of corn that would stretch across acres of fertile land. He was a proud man—not in an arrogant sense, but proud of his skills as a farmer and proud to pass that knowledge on to his lineage—even though he had no son. That was the type of man she wanted for a father to her children. Could she live with the other kind? Would it break her heart to see her children longing for attention from their father?

She could not give Ben an answer until she knew if he would be a good father or not. Being a provider was not enough; she wanted more. Not for herself, but for the children. She would not care if he never put a loving touch to her, but she wouldn't tolerate a violent one either. Nor could she accept a man who would not care for children in his charge in a loving way.

"I'm not sure I want to be married to a *mann* who is a stranger to his *kinner*. His *fraa* would be a different story, but wee ones don't understand that distance." Her statement was bold, but she'd meant every word.

"What about you, Eva?" she asked. "What is it you need?"

The answer was simple; if she married Ben, it would rid her of Adam, and it was possible she would be able to see Emily for Christmas without alerting her or anyone else that everything was exactly as it appeared—that they were a happy family expecting their first child together.

She'd found her answer; it wasn't what she'd expected, but it was an answer. It worried her that Ben hadn't ever held Grace, and if she had anything to say about it, that was about to change.

Chapter Twelve

Eva sat in front of the window and watched the snow fall in thick clumps. There had been a time in her life when such a day would send her reeling out the door to play in the wet, cold snow. She'd build a snowman and lie on the ground making snow angels, all the while, lying on her back with her mouth open just to catch a few flakes on her tongue.

Sitting here now, it was tough for her to do anything but sigh. She wasn't a child anymore; she was due to have a child of her own in a few months. Christmas was nearly upon them, and she had promised to give her answer to Ben tonight after dinner. If she consented, they would be married on Christmas Eve, just two days from today. Ben's friend, Ebner, and his wife, Anna, would be with them to celebrate Christmas with or without the wedding. They were Grace's kinfolk, and it made her a little nervous to think she could be scrutinized as the right choice for a mother to the child by people who had the power to take her away. From what the widow had told her, they already had three boys, and Anna was expecting twins to be born any day, and refused custody of Grace after Ellen's death because they didn't have the room for her.

Her stomach churned at the thought of being a wife and a mother, even though she was already a mother to Grace. Having her own child was a different story; it made her more nervous than an unbroken horse. Still, marrying Ben would be the only way she could keep her child, and still be a mother to Grace, with whom she'd fallen in love with.

Eva swallowed tears; how had her life become so out of control? Too many times she found herself wishing she'd never met Adam that night, but guilt tore at her for such thoughts. To regret what happened with Adam would be like wishing away her child, and she just couldn't do that no matter how it had come to life inside her. It wasn't the child's fault for how it came to be, and so the child should not have to suffer. But would it suffer if Adam ever found out it was his child? She prayed silently that the child would favor her looks instead of Adam's. perhaps if she had a daughter, the likelihood of it looking like her was higher than if she were to have a boy. Her heart sped up just thinking about having a son that looked like Adam.

Lord, forgive me for my worrisome thoughts, but I'm terrified of how I'll feel about mei boppli if it looks like Adam. Will I be able to love him? If it's your will, please let me have a dochder who looks like me or Emily. Bless me with the wisdom to make the right decision about marrying Ben; help me not to be afraid of him the way I am with Adam. I know he's never given me any reason not to trust him, but I'm still afraid. Give me courage and faith to trust. Danki

She closed her eyes against tears that relieved her one-by-one as each dropped—as if they'd drained her of every bit of worry that weighed on her. Within minutes, she opened her eyes and a feeling of peace washed over her as if she was standing under the waterfall at Willow Creek.

She leaned in and checked on Grace in her crib, kissing her on her warm cheek; the poor thing was worn out from staying up all night trying to cut her lower teeth.

"Sleep peacefully, sweetheart," she cooed. "Momma's going to go see your *dat* I'll be back before you wake."

Her heart swelled, a lump forming in her throat; it was the first time she'd allowed herself

to call herself *Momma*. It felt liberating—
exhilarating, even. She gazed upon her daughter
once more, a hand instinctively rolling across
her belly; soon she would have two *kinner*. *Gott*
had truly blessed her. She'd begged him for a
reason to live; being a mother was not the
answer she had expected the night her child was
conceived, the night that seemed suddenly so far
away.

In the mudroom, she found her cape on
the peg nearest the door. She pulled it around
her and tucked the sleeves of her sweater into
her mittens; then, she bundled up in her knit hat
and scarf. Stuffing her feet into her boots, she
shouldered out into the December morning with
a heart as light as the snow that fell all around
her.

Suddenly, she was free to act like a kid
again; she carefully lowered herself onto the
thick snow in the yard between the house and
the barn, leaning back and catching snowflakes
on her tongue. Swishing her arms and legs, she
made a snow angel. She lay there quietly,

thinking of her parents, and then of Emily. She missed them all; she wanted so much for Emily to be at her wedding. Did she dare expose her secret? Would she have to mislead her into believing the child she carried belonged to Ben?

She heard crunching snow and looked up, shielding her eyes against the drifting snow; Ben stood in front of her, a curious look on his face.

She smiled slowly and he smiled back; he was truly a handsome man. His chiseled jaw was peppered with a day's growth, which complimented his kind, blue eyes.

"It seems I've gotten myself a little stuck here," she said, trying to wiggle herself upright.

Ben pulled off his work glove and reached out his hand to assist her, the warmth of his fingers permeating her mitten sending tingles up her arm. She'd never experienced such an exciting sensation; Adam had never made her feel like that—not even when they were young and she was infatuated with him.

She hesitated, enjoying the warmth of his touch. "I think I'm content to sit here for a minute."

He plopped down in the snow beside her. "In that case, I think I'll join you. I suppose while I'm down here, I should make an angel for Ellen."

Eva was quiet as she watched him form the snow angel and look up into the heavens.

"She was a very lost soul, I'm afraid," he finally said. "I couldn't help her; I couldn't do anything for her except give her a *gut* name. She and I never had a connection. It was painfully awkward being married to her as rebellious as she was, but I was determined to protect her. She was the younger *schweschder* of *mei* best friend, and there was nothing more to it than that. She was a very beautiful woman—on the outside, but her inner beauty was severely lacking. She didn't want to marry me; she was in love with the *mann* who'd gotten her into trouble. She would have never loved me as a *fraa* should, but I was content with the sacrifice I'd made."

"What about me?" she asked. "What makes you think marrying me will be any different?"

"I know you're hurting because of your situation," he said slowly. "But I've seen the way you take care of Grace; you've made that wee one your own. Ellen never wanted the *boppli;* she thought marrying me would make her old boyfriend jealous, and when that didn't work, she thought he'd come get her for the sake of the child and he would come to his senses and realize suddenly how much they both meant to him. Even up to the moments after she gave birth; her first comments were how proud he'd be and jealous enough to come for her and the *boppli.*"

"*Ach,* I'm sorry," she said. "Did the *vadder* come for Grace?"

"*Nee,* two days after Ellen's funeral, he signed his rights to Grace over to me. I was at a loss; I couldn't give her away even though I had

157

no idea how to care for a *boppli*, but I didn't have the heart to put her in an orphanage. That's when *Gott* sent me an angel—you!"

She sat up and looked at him. "Me?"

"*Jah,* I'd prayed for someone who would love her the way a *mamm* should. I knew from the first time you held her you would never want to let her go."

Tears dripped from her eyes and he reached slowly and wiped at them with his thumb. His touch was so gentle and loving; how could she have ever thought he could be as monstrous as Adam?

"Don't cry; I don't ever want to make you cry," he said. "You're a beautiful woman inside and out, and the other *mann* has no idea what he's lost, but I'm glad that *Gott* opened the door for me."

Eva looked at him—truly looked into his serious but kind, blue eyes. How had God managed to answer all her prayers so fast? Was it because she was in such desperate need and willing to do His will? If she had not been open to God's plan for her life, she might just have missed out on this wonderful man and little Grace—what a double blessing.

He leaned up on his haunches in front of her, removed his other glove and cupped her face in his hands.

Her breath hitched and her lashes fluttered as he drew her face closer. His warm breath tickled her cold lips as they barely touched hers—as if he was waiting for permission.

Could she kiss this man and lose herself in him? She was willing to marry him, but not in name only. God had given her the courage and the desire to want a real marriage; did Ben want the same with her?

She inched toward him, lost in his tenderness, his lips sweeping across hers making her head swim with a delightful dizziness. She deepened the kiss, overwhelmed at the gentle passion that he held her with. He'd captured her heart in this one small moment—something

Adam hadn't been able to accomplish the entire time she'd known him.

Was it possible there was some level of love between them already? Perhaps not yet, but there was something certainly stirring between them and it was enough to make her want to accept his proposal. Love would come later; she was certain Ben would be an easy man to love.

He drew away from her gently at first, and then his countenance changed to a more serious demeanor.

"Will you marry me, then?" he asked abruptly.

"Are you asking out of obligation to secure a *mamm* for Grace?" she asked.

He shook his head, smiling. "I'm asking because I truly want to make a life with you," he said. "You're the answer to my prayers, and you're a fine woman. I don't need to know the details of what brought you to this place in your life, but I hope that one day you'll trust me enough to tell me about it."

"*Jah,* I'd like that too—but it might take some time."

"Take all the time you need; we have a lifetime to get to know each other—that is—if you'll have me as your husband and the *vadder* of your *kinner."*

"*Jah,* I'd like that very much," she said. "I'll marry you, Ben, and I'll raise Grace as my own *dochder."*

He smiled wide just before he pressed his lips to hers once more.

Eva stood before the Mennonite preacher, Ben at her right side. Her gaze met his as the preacher had him repeat his vows to her; the gleam in his eye told her how proud he was to take her as his wife. She was equally proud; she couldn't have asked God for a better man to spend the rest of her life with.

The child within her womb wriggled around, making her heart sing; she was doing the right thing for herself, her child, and for Grace.

"You may kiss your bride," the preacher said.

Ben dipped his head to meet her lips with his; it was a gentle and meaningful kiss that would likely stay with her for the rest of her life.

Afterward, her new family—Grace's family, greeted her and Ben with congratulatory hugs. Alma had not shown up, and that worried her, but she understood that her place needed to be with Emily. It was, after all, Christmas Eve, and she was grateful that her sister did not have to be alone.

After she had the baby, she would go back and present her husband and child to her sister, but until that time, distance was probably the best explanation for now. When all was said and done, she would go to her with a husband and play it off as though he was the father of her child. She didn't like deceiving her sister, and she would never deny Adam his right to the child if there was a chance he would be a good father, but the way that child came into being was enough for her to know the answer to that was a negative one.

"Let's eat," Widow Bontrager said to their guests.

The widow and Anna had been up most of the night preparing the meal for today; they'd both insisted Eva rested and worried about caring for Grace, while they did all the work. Guilt plagued her; she didn't want them to work too hard for her, but since she was well-rested for the ceremony, that almost made up for it.

A knock at the door startled from her thoughts. She opened the door and in hobbled Alma.

"What happened to you?" Eva whispered.

Alma leaned in close. "I'm sorry I wasn't here, but there's something you need to know."

"What's wrong?"

"It's Emily; Adam asked her to marry him and she's meeting him tonight to tell him yes!"

The blood drained from Eva's cheeks, a lump stuck in her throat where she strangled a cry. She clamped her hand over her mouth and looked over her shoulder to be sure Ben had not seen her reaction.

"I *have* to save her from making the biggest mistake of her life. What should I do?"

"Can you slip away from your *wedding*— I'm so sorry to have to pull you away from your wedding, but..."

"I know," Eva said, a cry still trying to escape. "But I'm sure he'll understand if I have to go to her and talk some sense into her. Are you okay to drive like that?"

"I slipped and fell on the icy sidewalk at your *mamm's* house when I ran out to my car," Alma answered. "I think I only sprained it, but it's the left foot and I don't need that to drive...I just can't put any pressure on it."

Eva took a deep breath; she hated to leave her new husband and family. Anna would be leaving first thing in the morning so she and

Ebner could visit with his family too for the season. They'd brought their boys with them so they could see their cousin, Grace. It had been a sweet family reunion, but Eva had an obligation to warn her sister about Adam before it was too late.

Surely, they would understand—wouldn't they?

Chapter Thirteen

Eva rehearsed in her head what she planned on saying to Emily and worried about how she would approach the subject of her pregnancy. She had to put that out of her mind for the time being. What was of utmost importance was getting her sister to see reason regarding Adam.

"What are you going to tell her when she asks about the baby?" Alma asked as she drove slowly over the snowy ribbons of road that led to Eva's childhood home. "And what if she's with Adam? What will you say to *him* about it?"

Eva turned away from the snow-covered landscape and looked at Alma. "I'll say I'm married to Ben," she answered. "He doesn't have to know I only just got married thirty minutes ago."

"I can't believe Ben let you go like that," Alma said. "He's a very understanding man— and so handsome; you better hold onto him!"

Eva giggled and blushed. "*Jah,* he is; he's so much the opposite of Adam, but he was just as concerned as I was when Emily didn't show up for the wedding. He thinks we need to talk it out; I think that's why he let me go. He's a *gut mann,* but he doesn't know any of the rest of this—he doesn't know what a monster Adam is, or he might not have let me go."

"You don't have to convince me of that," Alma said, turning her car into the driveway and stopping at the end. "Get Emily to see it; I begged her to talk to you, first, but she said she had nothing to say to you. She knows you just got married; what if she tells Adam?"

"I'll worry about that if it comes up. Right now, I have to fight her silence against me. She only refused to talk to me because she knows I'll try to talk her out of it—but for different reasons than what she thinks."

Eva took a deep breath; the two-hour drive there had gone by too fast, and now she faced having to reveal her secrets to her sister. She'd hoped to avoid such a talk with her, but it seemed it was the only way to make her believe what a danger Adam was to her.

Lord, give me strength and wisdom to help Emily before it's too late.

Eva reached for the door handle and pulled it open, but Alma's hand on her arm stopped her.

"There's something else you should know before you see Emily," she said.

Eva face turned cold as the blood drained from her cheeks. The stricken look on Alma's face set off an internal alarm that made her shake uncontrollably.

"She has a bruise on her cheek," Alma admitted.

Eva's breath hitched and she put a gloved hand up to her mouth to cover it.

"When I asked her how she got the bruise on her face, she told me to mind my own business."

"It sounds like he's hitting her," Eva cried. "If he's being violent with her, why would she accept his marriage proposal?"

Alma sighed. "I asked her the same thing and she told me she didn't want to take care of the farm alone, and his proposal was likely the only one she'd ever get so she isn't about to turn it down. She thinks Adam is her only choice."

"She never did have much confidence; how am I going to convince her without telling her *everything?*"

Alma shrugged. "You might not be able to convince her no matter what you say."

"I have to try," she said, shouldering out into the cold night. "I'll be right back; keep the heater on."

Alma nodded.

Eva trod slowly over the snow-drifted walkway, the deep snow crunching beneath her feet. She paused before knocking on the front door; it seemed foreign to her, but she didn't have permission to walk in unannounced. She'd been gone too long, and it was no longer her home to enter without an invitation from her sister, and she didn't believe she would get one.

Emily opened the door and peered out, the chain keeping Eva from entering.

"What do you want?" Emily asked, her tone dripping with contempt. "Shouldn't you be at your wedding?"

"I got married a couple of hours ago."

"Then what are you doing here? I told Alma I didn't want to come to your wedding; I want nothing to do with you. You abandoned me and *mamm* so you could go have a better life somewhere else."

"That's not how it was," Eva pleaded. "Please let me in so I can talk to you."

Emily closed the door, slid the chain back and opened the door again. She turned her back and walked toward the kitchen in the back of the house.

Eva stomped the snow from her boots and walked into her childhood home. She stood in the entrance, breathing in the familiar smells of burning chicory in the fireplace, a hint of cinnamon coming from the kitchen. On the mantel, a pine wreath with pinecones reminded her of the ones made as they were growing up, and the popcorn strings they made to hang from the banister in loops with pine branches.

She followed Emily into the kitchen; she took a deep breath and let it out with a whoosh. Emily kept her back to her, putting away dishes that looked as if they'd been washed several hours ago.

"Did you have company for Christmas dinner?" Eva asked. She didn't know what else to say.

"Only Adam," Emily answered.

"Without an escort?"

Emily turned around and smirked. "I'm about to be married to him—New Year's Eve."

Eva gasped. "Please tell me you aren't marrying him, Em," she said.

"Why shouldn't I? He's handsome and funny and very much a gentleman," Emily said.

Eva guffawed. "Adam Byler is *no* gentleman!"

"Maybe he is with a real *lady*," Emily said.

Eva closed the space between them so she could look her sister in the eye. "Just what do you mean by that?"

"I think it's pretty self-explanatory, Eva," she said over her shoulder as she stacked the clean dinner plates in the cupboard. "It's obvious you left him for another *mann*."

"I'm warning you to stay away from Adam before you get hurt," Eva said, clenching her jaw. "You have no idea what Adam is really like; he drinks and he has a temper when he's been drinking."

"You're a jealous liar!" Emily accused without looking at her. "You don't want him, but you don't want me to have him either. You got married today—why would you care who Adam marries?"

"Because he's no *gut* for you."

"That's for me to decide—not you," Emily said, walking toward the back door. "You want everything for yourself. Maybe I want something more out of life than working this farm while you have your perfect life."

Eva scoffed. "You think my life is perfect? You have *no* idea how my life is."

Emily pushed her sleeves into her coat. "If you hadn't run off, you could have married

Adam and had a life here instead of leaving me all alone. Adam is the only one who cares about me right now."

"I *had* to leave the community—to get away from Adam and his violence against me. From the look of your cheek, I'd say he's still drinking and taking his aggression out on *you* now!"

Emily drew her hand to her cheek and covered the bruise. "I knocked the shovel off the wall in the barn and it hit me in the face."

"That's the same sort of story I used to make up whenever Adam would hit me," Eva said, tears clogging her throat. "Please listen to me, Em, before it's too late and you live to regret it the way I did."

"I won't listen to another lie about Adam," she said, grabbing her mittens and hat. "I'm going to be late meeting him and I won't make him wait for me."

"He didn't wait for me!" Eva said, raising her voice.

Emily turned on her heels and leered at her sister. "What is that supposed to mean? You're the one who broke it off with him, remember?"

"I mean...he didn't wait for..." her voice trailed off and she paused too long.

Emily grabbed a flashlight and swung open the kitchen door, running out into the snowy night before Eva could find her voice to stop her.

Chapter Fourteen

Eva's heart nearly dropped to her shoes; she was helpless to stop her sister from walking out on their conversation. She had so much to tell her, so much to warn her about. Why hadn't she been able to get the words out? If she had, maybe Emily would have understood what she was trying so hard to warn her about.

Eva pulled open the kitchen drawer for some matches; she'd have to take the lantern to go after Emily. It was too dark to see unless she got lucky and the clouds made a clearing for the full moon. She couldn't take that chance; she had to stop Emily and there was no time to lose.

In the driveway, she went out to the car to tell Alma what she was doing. She rolled down the window.

"I have to go after Em; she took off toward the covered bridge over Deadman's Ravine to meet Adam."

"Are you talking about Peace River?" Alma asked.

Eva nodded. "Can you drive over there and meet me; it'll take you about five minutes to get over there by car because you have to go all the way around since they blocked it off when they condemned the bridge. You'll have to go over to County Road 17 North."

"It's going to take me close to fifteen minutes to get over there by car; I'll have to drive slow around those icy curves."

"Unless you think you can walk with me over the footpath through the field."

Alma shook her head. "I don't think I'll make it on this ankle; the cold is making it throb. Go after her; I won't be far behind you, but be careful."

"I will," Eva said, lighting the lantern.

She walked to the back of the property and started trudging through the cornfield. Short, untilled cornstalks formed rows along the path; they were like sharp, icy knives jutting up from the earth. The wind-blown furrows outlined in black earth and crisp, white snow formed pattern in the field. The dirt was packed frozen and rough to walk over, but she hurried through the dangerous maze until she reached the middle; there, she stopped in her tracks.

From the corner of her eye, she spotted someone coming across the field; it was a silhouette of a man—a tall man in a black suit and black hat. She stifled a cry that gurgled from her diaphragm and up through her throat, threatening to paralyze her. She quickened her pace, fearing it was Adam. She was too far from home to turn back, but it wouldn't matter; there was no one there to protect her from him. Her only choice was to keep moving forward and hope Alma would reach the bridge before her.

Her heart pounded in her ears, the whistling of the wind drowning it out only a little. She stumbled, cutting her knee on an icy cornstalk poking up from the frozen field. She didn't dare look back, her eyes bulging and her ears perked. Was he following her? Would he quicken his pace to reach her before she could get help?

"Lord, help me!" she blubbered.

Memories of that day flooded her mind; the day after, when she'd stumbled through this same field. Five months had passed since that day, but the memory of it still paralyzed her. She tucked a hand under her swelled abdomen as if to cradle her baby. She would protect that baby—even from its own father if need be. Tears ran down her cheeks stinging as they froze there, her heavy breaths making puffs of icy air blow out in front of her.

The bridge was only a few steps away now and she could see the single beam glowing from Emily's flashlight. Emily was there inside the bridge, but she didn't see Adam's buggy from across the other side. Her blood ran through her veins with an icy chill; had he been behind her the whole time? She looked back, and indeed, it was him sauntering toward her, but he was in no hurry—he liked the game of it. He was still far enough back that she had time to warn Emily if she hurried.

She walked swiftly, yet cautiously, making sure she didn't slip on the icy snow. Adam would take his time as usual; he seemed to enjoy the hunt almost as much as the catch.

"Em," she said, closing the space between them. "Hurry, we need to get to the other side of the bridge; Adam's coming up behind me."

Emily looked beyond her sister and scrunched up her face. "Are you losing your mind, Eva? There's no one behind you! Adam lives that way," she said, pointing the opposite direction.

"I know where he lives," she said impatiently, checking behind her again. Where had he gone? Surely, she wasn't losing her mind; he was there—she'd seen him.

"He was there, I'm telling you! We have to get out of here. Please trust me, Em."

Emily turned her back on her and looked out at the water rushing under the bridge. The wind whipped heavy snowflakes that pelted them in the face, even from inside the open bridge. The water was choppy tonight and had risen several feet from rainfall since late summer, the last time she'd been here.

She shuddered as her gaze fell upon the spot where she'd woken the morning after. She pushed her cape to the side, watching Emily's gaze as it drew toward her protruding belly.

"Adam did this to me!" Eva said through gritted teeth. "Is this what you want from him?"

"I don't believe you," Emily said. "Adam would not be *loose* with you."

"This wasn't some barn-romping, Em," she said. "Adam *forced* himself on me and left me for dead—right here on the floor of this bridge. Now, I'm pregnant—that's why I married Ben—so I could raise the *boppli*."

Emily clamped a hand over her mouth and shook her head, tears welling up in her eyes.

"You're lying!" she managed. "Adam wouldn't do that."

"Oh, but I did!"

Adam's voice sent a chill down Eva's spine, her limbs shaking uncontrollably as he emerged from the shadows of the far end of the bridge. How had he gotten there without her noticing?

"Adam," Emily greeted him with a shaky voice. "Eva didn't mean to say that about you; don't pay any attention to her."

He shook his head and closed the space between them, his jaw set, his eyes twinkling with a madness Eva knew too well.

She tried to move, but her wobbly legs betrayed her. A strangled cry emerged from her throat giving away her feelings. The delight in his eyes made her wish she'd not have come here.

"Did you think you could keep my *kinner* from me? I'm not going to let another *mann* raise my flesh and blood!" Adam said.

Eva gulped; she hadn't wanted him to know about the baby. She forced her left foot to the side, then her right; she couldn't make her feet move fast enough, but she needed to close the gap between herself and Emily. They'd make a run for it if they could; it might be their only chance.

Adam slid between them. "Not so fast! I came here for something and I'm going to take it; you're welcome to stay and watch, Eva!"

"No!" Eva screamed.

Emily tried to back away from him but he grabbed her and kissed her forcefully on the mouth. She batted at him and pushed him away, but he held her close. Eva rushed him, but he was too strong. He twisted her arm until it snapped. Her scream rent the air, echoing over the ravine in the icy, night air.

She tucked her arm in close to her, the pain bringing bile to her throat. She hung her head over the edge of the bridge and emptied the contents of her stomach. A scream from Emily brought her head back up. Adam struck her sister in the face a second time after she begged him to stop; this time, the force of the blow knocked her to the floor of the bridge in a heap, her sobs shaking her.

With her arm tucked in close, a rush of adrenaline forced Eva forward; protecting Emily from Adam drove her to rush toward him. Adam caught her by the throat before she could reach her sister.

She kicked at him, the pain in her arm nearly stealing her conscious mind from her.

Dizziness overcame her, but Emily rose from the floor and came to her defense.

Frau Byler let a gasp escape her lips as she watched her son fighting with the Yoder sisters. Their voices had been muffled by the thick snow that blanketed the wooded area with a silence that drowned out all outside noises. Had she heard Eva correctly? She'd accused Adam of violating her and impregnating her. She'd witnessed the girl lifting the folds of her cape and revealing her swelled abdomen. Adam had become enraged and it all happened so fast, she didn't have time to react.

She continued to watch from the other side of the bridge, tears welling up in her eyes at the realization that her son was just like his father. She wept quietly, her tears stinging the scrape on her cheek from her recent fight with the Bishop. She'd run from the house after he'd hit her several times. She wiped at her nose; it was still bleeding. Watching her son and listening to his temper put a distance between them. She had raised him to respect women, but it was obvious to her that he'd taken after his father.

He hadn't even denied Eva's accusations; he'd merely laughed at her and pushed at her. Even as his mother, *Frau* Byler was helpless to prevent her son from being a cruel man. What could she do to stop him? She hadn't been able to stop his father from abusing her for more than twenty years. She moved closer, wondering if she had the courage to step between her son and the two young women.

Gott, please help them; I'm too afraid.

"Let go, Adam!" Emily cried. "You're hurting her."

He gritted his teeth and smiled wickedly. "I haven't even begun to hurt her!"

He swung his arm in a wide arc, backhanding Emily in the face so hard she stumbled backward and hit her head on one of the beams inside the bridge. Her head wavered and her eyes rolled, and then she collapsed into a heap on the ground. Eva drew her hands to her mouth and screamed.

Adam stood between them, but Eva tried to push past him. He grabbed her by the throat with one hand and brought her close to his face. Alcohol soured his breath, his eyes glazed. She squirmed, but her arm prevented her from getting away.

"Do you think I'm going to let the two of you turn me into the police so I can go to jail because you're a jezebel and a tease?"

"I've kept your secret," she whispered, his grip on her throat cutting off her air.

Her heart beat wildly as his eyes grew wide. He was going to kill her if she could not get away; she was sure of it—his eyes told her everything.

He reached a hand inside her cape and ran his hand over her abdomen, his touch gagging her. "That's my flesh and blood you're carrying, and I won't let you take it from me!"

Breaking free, she backed up against the open window of the bridge. "I don't want you anywhere near *mei boppli.*"

Adam rushed at her, growling with anger, but she moved to the side to avoid him. He lost his footing on a patch of ice, his body lurching forward. He braced his hands against the window frame in vain, trying to catch himself, but the rotted wood of the ledge gave way and he toppled out with a whoosh.

His scream faded slowly as if paused in time until the thump and splash of his body hitting the water and rocks below echoed up from the ravine.

Eva shook as she stepped over to the window and looked down at his motionless body, a scream from the other side of the bridge startling her. Eva turned slowly toward *Frau* Byler, who was screaming a mournful cry, her face was bruised and blood dripped from her nose.

Eva stepped toward her, reaching out to her but she drew back, shaking her head and crying in short bursts. The woman stared past her. "You killed him," she said barely above a whisper.

"It was an accident!" Eva cried, adrenaline surging through like ice water and pooling in the soles of her feet, paralyzing her there.

Chapter Fifteen

Eva clamped a hand over her mouth to stifle her cries as Adam's mother turned and walked away in the direction of her home. She hadn't pushed Adam; had it looked that way to his mother from where she'd been standing?

"Please," she called out to her. "I didn't kill him; you have to believe me!"

Frau Byler didn't look back, but hurried her steps, her cries fading the further into the wooded path she walked.

A groan from Emily brought Eva back to reality. She rushed to her side, relieved that she was conscious and breathing. "Don't move; I'll get help," she said to her sister, icy tears stinging her cheeks.

She looked up toward the road, a set of headlights lighting up the eerie darkness, the low rumbling of her cousin's muffler becoming louder as she approached. Relief washed over her, forcing a sob to escape amid her blubbering.

She left Emily's side and hurried to meet Alma. Drawing in a ragged breath, she rushed to her car sobbing uncontrollably, a rush of emotion overcoming her.

She collapsed into Alma's arms the minute she exited the car.

"What happened?"

"Adam's dead," she cried. "Adam's dead and his mother thinks I killed him."

Alma dropped her arms and fell back against the car, her hands drawn to her face.

"What do you mean, she thinks you killed him? Was she here—wait—*did* you kill him?"

"Of course, not," Eva sobbed. "It was an accident."

"He's really dead?" she asked.

Eva nodded.

"Where is he? How did it happen?"

Eva pointed toward the bridge. "He fell— out of the window."

She shivered and her teeth chattered. The wind blew icy flakes against her damp cheeks, stinging them. She drew her mitten-clad hands to her face and blew out a breath with a long whoosh.

"What am I going to do, Alma?"

"If he *fell,* then let's get out of here!"

"I can't just leave him here!" Eva cried.

"Why not?" she asked. "He left you, didn't he?"

Alma tucked her arm in Eva's, causing her to let out a scream; she doubled over from the pain.

"What's wrong?"

"Adam—he broke my arm, I think."

Alma reached for her arm with a gentle touch. "I'm so sorry, Eva, I didn't know."

"I know you didn't," she said letting out another long deep breath. "I need you to help me get Emily into the car. Adam knocked her silly and she's half-passed out on the floor of the bridge."

"Oh my gosh!"

They walked over the bridge, Alma stepped slowly to the side where Adam's fall had broken the wooden wall. She stood there looking down and then pointed. She waved Eva over toward the window. "Hey, there's someone walking down there to him; isn't that the Bishop?"

Eva's heart raced, a bead of sweat rolling down the middle of her back despite the rigid cold of the night. "Oh no! What am I going to tell him? I've got to get out of here."

"We can't, Eva, it's too late," Alma said. "Adam's mother saw you here; she accused you of killing him. She'll tell the police the same thing."

She pulled her cell phone out of her coat pocket and handed it to Eva. "If you call the police it'll go a long way to making you look like you're not guilty; real murderers don't call the police on themselves."

Eva's lips trembled, fear coursing through her veins like a bolt of lightning. "What if they don't believe me? What if his *mamm* tells them she *saw* me do it?"

"Emily's a witness, too," Alma said.

A groan startled her gaze from Adam's lifeless body. She shook her head; the blood draining from her face.

"Em was passed out before he fell, so she didn't see it happen," Eva whimpered, her knees buckling under her. "My only witness is his mother, and she thinks I killed him!"

Alma let Eva lean against her; she was shaking so violently her head hurt. "What am I going to do?"

Alma pushed 911 into her phone and handed it to Eva. "You tell the truth and then you pray."

"911, what's your emergency?" the person on the other end of the line answered.

"*Ach,* the Bishop's son fell off the bridge," Eva blurted out, her accent so thick she could scarcely recognize her own voice.

"Which bridge, Miss," the woman asked.

"*Deadman's...*" Eva's heart raced. "I—I mean, Peace River; the covered bridge on County Road 17, North."

"How badly is he hurt, Miss?"

"I don't know; he hasn't moved," she said. "I—I think he's—*dead.*"

"I'm dispatching an ambulance now," the operator said. "What is your name, Miss?'

"Eva Yoder—Eva Bontrager—I just got married." She had no idea why she was rambling so much; it was tough enough to keep her voice steady enough for the woman to understand her.

"Can you tell me the deceased's name," the woman said, her voice monotone.

"I—I don't even know if he's dead," Eva admitted.

"His name please."

"Adam Byler; he fell from the bridge, but I don't know if he's dead or not because I can't get down the ravine to see—it's too steep and icy."

"I'm sending a search and rescue team as well; they'll be able to retrieve his body. Don't try to go down there if it isn't safe; wait for the officers to get there."

"Officers?" Eva asked, her heart hammering like a woodpecker.

"They'll have to take your statement," the operator said. "So, you'll need to stay there until they arrive."

"I hear the sirens now," Eva blubbered.

"I'm going to let you go so you can show them where the body is," she said.

Eva gulped. She hadn't thought of Adam as deceased, or as a *body*. He was most likely dead and she wasn't certain how she felt about it other than relief, and that made her feel awful.

There were so many times she might have wished him dead after what he did to her—but then she'd forgiven him finally and moved on with her life. Only God had the right to decide if he should live or die, but she wondered if he'd had enough time to think about repenting before he hit the bottom of the ravine? She shook away the awful thought and pulled in a deep breath of icy air. It made her cough, but the siren from the approaching ambulance made her shake.

Emily rose from the floor of the bridge with assistance from Alma. "Are you alright,

Eva?" she asked. "I heard you screaming but I couldn't get up from the ground; I felt like I was dreaming or something."

"I think my arm is broken, and I'm shaken up; how are you feeling? I was so afraid, I thought he was going to kill us both."

Emily hugged her sister. "I'm so sorry for accusing you of being jealous; you were right about him." She rubbed at her throat. "He tried to choke me to death; thank you for helping me. I wouldn't have blamed you if you didn't. I'm sorry about what he did to you—about the *boppli.*"

"I hope you understand now why I couldn't come home."

Emily nodded. "I wish you would have told me what he did; of course, I probably wouldn't have believed you. He sure had me blinded to his evilness."

The ambulance pulled up to the other side of the bridge, followed by a firetruck and two police cars.

Eva shook, her teeth chattering more from nerves than the weather.

"Let's go tell them what happened so you can get home to that new husband and daughter," Emily said with an encouraging smile. "I can't wait to meet them."

Eva forced a smile. "I can't wait to show them off—but let's get through this first; I can't decide if I feel more like throwing up or passing out right now."

They took a step toward the police officers, but they all stopped to watch the Bishop dragging Adam's body up the side of the ravine. Her breath hitched, sobs clogging her throat. She ducked back into the shadows of the bridge, holding her hand over her mouth so stifle her cries. From there, she could see Adam's bloody face, his legs mangled and broken; from the way his head was flopped to one side, she'd guess his neck was also broken.

The sobs in her throat burst out at the sight of the Bishop struggling with him until he reached level ground.

Her gaze locked with the Bishop's, his face twisting angrily. Instinct made her want to bolt, but she didn't have the strength to move.

Paramedics rushed over to him with a gurney and lifted Adam's lifeless body onto it. They pulled the sheet over his face, she assumed they didn't think taking his pulse was even worth the time.

They stood there with sober looks on their faces and the Bishop pointed to Eva, his fiery glare sending a race of adrenaline through her so fast, it made her feet burn.

"Murderer!" he yelled, pointing at Eva. "Arrest that Jezebel; she murdered my son."

Chapter Sixteen

"I didn't do it," Eva cried. "It was an accident."

Eva tucked her arm close to keep it as still as possible, despite the tremors violently shaking her. Ben had asked to tag along, and now she wished she'd let him. Even Alma hadn't been here to witness against the Bishop's accusations, and unless his wife stopped telling the same lies, Eva was going to jail. She could see it in the officer's expression. Eva shook so violently it frightened her. She'd never been to jail before but she'd heard plenty of stories about it from Priscilla's last boyfriend who'd gotten into some trouble as a teen. Jail was no place for a pregnant woman; they would take her child away from her after it was born. She took a deep breath and pushed down her worrying thoughts. If she wasn't calm, she would make herself look guilty.

Two of the officers took the Bishop aside so they could take his statement away from Eva. He walked past her and his gaze locked on hers, his eyes were red-rimmed. If not for the evil heart the man shared with his son, Eva would almost feel sorry for him. He was determined to make her pay for the loss of his son, but in reality, he was mostly to blame. From what she could see, he'd set a bad example for his son by abusing Adam's mother in front of him his entire life.

The officer in front of her began to jot down notes on a notepad and then looked up at her. "Now tell me what happened here tonight," he said.

Eva whimpered and cradling her arm.

Alma put a hand up to stop the officer's questions. "She needs a paramedic to look at her arm; Adam twisted it and we think it's broken."

The officer nodded to the paramedics, waving them over to Eva, and then went back to jotting things down on his notepad.

He looked up briefly. "So, the two of you were fighting, is that right?"

Eva nodded, her breath hitching from all the crying.

"Is that when you pushed him from the bridge?" The officer said.

Eva sucked in a breath. "*Nee*—no!" she cried. "I told you I didn't push him; he was trying to grab me again and he slipped on a patch of ice. He fell against the bridge at the window, and he tried to brace himself, but the wood on the bridge is so rotted that he fell through because the wood broke away."

The officer held up a hand to the paramedic to stop what he was doing. "Can you show me the patch of ice?"

Eva nodded and pointed. "It's right in front of the broken window."

They all walked inside the bridge and over to the spot that had broken away. Eva pointed to the large icy puddle right in front of the place where Adam fell. She prayed that it would be enough to show the officer that Adam's death was an accident, but his pursed lips and subtle nod made her uneasy.

"Let's go to the ambulance so they can look at your arm in the light and we can finish our talk there," the officer said.

As they walked past the Bishop he began to flail his arms at her. "Murderer! You murdered my son."

He flailed his arms and took an aggressive step toward Eva, but the officer restrained him. His eyes were filled with a fiery anger, and if not for the officer's presence, he might have caused her physical harm. She fully believed that the bruises on his wife's face and her bloodied nose were the result of a beating she'd suffered before she'd ventured out toward the bridge tonight. If not for that, she would have asked what the woman was doing out there wandering around in the dark all alone. Perhaps she'd known that her son was meeting with Emily tonight, giving her cause to worry. Surely, she had to know that her son was just like her husband.

The paramedics made her comfortable on the gurney inside the ambulance while the officer stood at the tailgate with Alma. She whimpered while they examined her arm, occasionally letting a yelp escape her lips if they moved it wrong. They slipped a plastic sleeve over her arm and filled it with air from a small compressor. She winced a little from the pressure but once she got used to it, it was easier to move without risking bumping it on something. While they eased it into a sling, the other officer approached the ambulance and they began conversing quietly.

The other officer looked beyond her at the paramedics who were working to make her comfortable. "Are you finished with her here, or do you need to transport her to the hospital?"

The young man nodded to the officer and then shrugged. "I don't see any reason to take her to the hospital."

The officer looked Eva straight in the eye. "I'm afraid we have an eyewitness who states you murdered Adam Byler; I have no choice but to place you under arrest for suspicion of murder. Eva Bontrager, you have the right to remain silent. Anything you say..."

Eva screamed and grabbed her side, the pain almost unbearable. She pulled in a deep breath, followed by a series of pants and then blowing out a long breath with a whoosh.

One of the paramedics grabbed a fetal doppler and then asked her to lie back on the gurney. The paramedics from the other ambulance wheeled Adam's mangled body past them. She whimpered and panted, dizziness overcoming her.

She clamped her left hand over her mouth.

"I'm going to throw up!"

A paramedic grabbed a basin and put it in front of her just in time; she choked and sputtered as she emptied the contents of her stomach. He took the basin from her, offered her a tissue, and then grabbed a water bottle off the shelf and handed it to her.

She wiped the cold sweat from her brow with the back of her hand. Tears filled her eyes and she let out another long groan. "Am I going to lose the *boppli?*"

The older paramedic draped a sheet over her. "Will you let me listen for a heartbeat?"

She nodded and he exposed a small area of her abdomen just above the sheet. "This is going to be a little bit cold," he said as he squirted gel on the end of the probe.

He placed it on her skin and she jumped; it *was* cold. But despite her pain, she remained very still. Within seconds, a rhythmic thumping resounded from the speaker on the device.

"It sounds good and strong, but a little fast," he said. "It's possible that the baby is in distress."

He looked up at the officer. "Will need to transport her to the hospital," he said. "At the very least, she'll need an ultrasound to make sure the placenta is still intact and that her water hasn't broken."

The officer nodded, his jaw set. "I'll need to ride along; this woman is my prisoner and she needs to be guarded."

The officer climbed into the back of the ambulance, and Eva began to sob harder.

"I'll follow behind," his partner said just before he closed the ambulance door.

"Wait!" Eva said.

He opened the door a little bit. "What do you need?"

"I need to talk to my sister and my cousin," Eva sobbed.

The officer narrowed his eyes. "Make it fast!"

Eva looked at her family. "Someone needs to go and tell Ben where I am so he won't worry."

"I don't want to leave you," Emily cried.

Eva shook her head wincing from the sharp pains in her side. "I need you to go with Alma; help her convince Ben not to come to see me, but let him know that I'm alright."

The officer shut the door and then slapped at it with an open hand twice to signal the driver he was clear to go.

Eva relaxed her head back on the gurney, her mournful sobs turning to angry tears.

The older paramedic put a hand on her shoulder, while the other one worked to put an IV in her arm. "Try to relax as best you can; it's not good for you to be this stressed out, and it's even worse on the baby."

She turned her head away from the officer and closed her eyes, the pain being all she could concentrate on at the moment. Still, her mind reeled with ideas about how she was going to stay out of jail long enough to get Adam's mother to tell the truth about what happened. She supposed the woman had to be afraid of what the Bishop would do to her if she defended Eva. She shuddered to think about what being in jail would do to her and the child she carried.

Her thoughts suddenly turned to Ben; what would he think of her when he learned the news. Would he still love her and want to stay married to her after he discovered she was being accused of murder?

Lord, please cover me with a hedge of protection; don't let them put me in jail for something I didn't do. Bless Frau Byler with courage and conviction to tell the truth about what happened to her son.

The paramedics wheeled her in through the emergency room quickly, the jostling making her side ache so intensely she cried out. Alma and Emily ran through the parking lot toward them, but the officers ushered them toward a waiting room. She was a prisoner now; the offer had called her a prisoner, and she would likely not be allowed to see them.

"We'll go talk to Ben instead of waiting here," Alma called to her.

She didn't have the strength to respond, but more than that, she didn't want them there seeing her guarded like a criminal.

From the corner of her eye she caught the other ambulance drivers wheeling the gurney covered with a sheet; Adam's body was beneath that sheet.

"Why did they bring him to the hospital?"

Was that her voice?

"The morgue is in the basement," the officer said. "They'll need to declare him officially deceased before we can officially charge you."

Murder.

She could still hear his scream in her mind and the duet of screams from his mother as he fell into the ravine. She'd prayed it away the entire trip to the hospital, but it would not leave her.

Would it haunt her forever?

Chapter Seventeen

Eva tried to relax, hoping the medicine they were pumping into her veins would stop the contractions. It was difficult for her to stay calm, considering how painful they were. The fact that she had an armed guard just outside the door of her hospital room did not help her nerves any.

She breathed through them the way the nurse had instructed her, but it was still almost unbearable. Would it be that way when it came time to give birth later? How had her mother stood the pain of giving birth to two children; no wonder it had weakened Grace's mother to the point of death. From what Ben had described, she'd not eaten much and had become severely depressed after Grace's father had rejected her, and had in turn, become too weak to give birth. Under normal healthy circumstances, Eva could see where it would be a strain, and the nurse had assured her the pains would only increase once real labor began.

The very idea of it frightened her.

Never mind that the nurse had told her that the minute she held her baby in her arms, the pains would immediately be forgotten. She wasn't convinced.

The door to her room opened slowly, and Ben peeked his head in.

"Can I come in?" he asked with a genuine smile.

An unexpected sob escaped her at the sight of him; she had been worried for the past few hours that he would not want to see her again, but seeing his smile put her at ease more than the medicine.

She nodded, her lower lip quivering.

He rushed to her side and pulled her into his arms, allowing her to sob freely. He shushed her gently, kissing the top of her head. "It's alright; Emily and Alma filled me in on most of what happened and I'm here now. I should have never let you go alone; I'm so sorry for not being there to protect you."

"I wish you could have been there to protect me from him before he had a chance to force himself on me," she cried. "Maybe then I wouldn't be in this mess."

She let out a groan and began to breathe heavily. Ben held her hands tightly and began to breathe with her until the contraction subsided.

"How long have you been in labor?"

"Ever since they arrested me!" She sobbed.

"I suspected he hurt you and took advantage of you," Ben said. "You didn't strike me as the type of woman who would give herself to a man out of wedlock. Is there anything you can tell the police that would make them understand his death was an accident? If he was physically hurting you at the time of the accident, I believe they would consider that self-defense."

"I was afraid to talk to the police after it happened because I didn't think they would believe me. He's the Bishop's son."

Ben caressed her cheek affectionately and kissed her on the forehead. "In the community, he was the Bishop's son, but in the English world he is no different than anyone else. The detective said he would give me a few minutes alone with you and then he wanted to speak with you; I think it's important that you tell him everything. I'll be right here by your side. Adam can't hurt you physically anymore but his death can cause you a great deal of harm if you don't defend yourself and open up about what he did."

Eva wiped her face and blew her nose with the tissues on the table near her hospital bed. She looked her new husband straight in the eye drawing courage from his willingness to help her and get the truth out in the open once and for all.

"I'm ready now," she said with one last sniffle. "Send him in; I'll tell him everything."

Eva wrung her hands and said a little prayer in her head asking for strength and the courage to open up about Adam's crimes against her.

A man she hadn't seen yet walked into her room alongside her husband and introduced himself as Detective Bartlett. He pulled up a chair near her bed. "I'll be brief," he said. "Your doctor has given me permission to speak with you and take your statement if necessary as long as your blood pressure stays low. I know this is all very difficult for you, but I'll need you to stay calm so we can get through this quickly and painlessly. I have a few questions to ask you and you don't have to answer me, but it might help you if you cooperate with me so we can try to keep you out of jail."

Eva nodded. She would give him whatever information she could in order to keep from going to jail.

"I understand you were married earlier today," he said. "Is that correct?"

"*Jah,*" she said.

He pointed to Ben. "Is he your husband?"

"*Jah,*" she repeated.

"If you are just married, what were you doing out at the bridge?"

"I went there to tell my sister the truth about what happened between Adam and me and to plead with her to stay away from him. I was afraid he would hurt her in the same way that he'd hurt me; he threatened me that he would hurt her if I told anyone what he did to me."

"Is Adam Byler the father of the child you're carrying?" he asked.

She nodded. "*Jah.*"

He paused to jot down some notes on the pad of paper in his hand and then looked up thoughtfully. "Were you a willing participant in that conception?"

"What do you mean?" she asked.

"Did he force himself on you? Is that how you became pregnant?"

She nodded without looking up at him.

"Is there any evidence to substantiate your claim?" the detective asked.

"I don't understand," Eva said, letting her accent roll thickly off her tongue, hoping he would explain things well enough for her to understand his questions.

"Were there any witnesses, or perhaps, something that would link the two of you that could prove your accusations against him."

She shrugged. "Such as what? I'm not sure I understand the question."

He took in a deep breath and lowered his gaze. "Let me explain this as delicately as possible because the last thing I want to do is upset you and cause you to have a miscarriage. In cases like these it's always best to see a doctor immediately so he can collect *certain evidence,* but since it's been so many months since the incident and you've obviously showered multiple times and likely laundered your clothing or disposed of it, we have to stretch a little further to look for evidence."

Eva leaned her head back and closed her eyes, retracing her steps that morning no matter how much the memories caused her to shake. She'd hidden herself away from her family, feeling ashamed over Adam's sins against her. She had done nothing to encourage Adam's behavior, yet his shameful acts against her had caused her to cower and hide as if she had in some way been partly to blame for what he'd done to her.

Though she'd used poor judgment in meeting him at such a late hour, he should have respected her after she'd rejected his advances toward her. He hadn't respected her, and for that, he would face judgment in the afterlife. It was not her place to judge him, only to forgive him—not for his sake, but for hers.

The memory of her bruises and the pain she'd experienced both physically and mentally caused her to break down. She'd bathed that morning, washing away all the evidence, but there was something that nagged at her. She hadn't disposed of her clothing; she'd hung it up on the back of the bathroom door in the *dawdi haus*.

Would it even still be there? It had been so long ago that Emily had likely found her apron and laundered it since then.

"That morning I wasn't thinking clearly; I left my apron hanging on the hook on the back of the door of the bathroom. It's in the *dawdi haus* at my parent's property. In the pocket, I remember putting my *underwear* in the pocket because—because..." She began to sob all over again, causing the monitor at her bedside to beep, her blood pressure rising out of control.

The detective stood. "Tell me why you put them in the pocket of your apron."

"Because when I woke up the next morning on the floor of the covered bridge," she sobbed. "They were torn and wrapped around my ankle."

She buried her face and her husband's shoulder and sobbed while several nurses entered the room to check on her.

The detective turned to the officer beside him. "Run down to the basement to the morgue and tell them to collect DNA samples from the deceased."

Eva felt a cold hand clamp over her mouth. She tried to scream but she could barely breathe around his strong hand. She struggled to pull in air around his steely grip, her gaze wide on the Bishop's angry eyes.

"Don't you make a sound, you little Jezebel," he threatened her. "I can't let you drag my *gut* name and that of my son's through the mud with your filthy lies about him. I know you teased him until he couldn't take it any longer and finally gave in to your unholy seduction—that's why you're carrying his seed inside you."

She buckled against the pain of a contraction; she hadn't had one in a while and she supposed she'd drifted off to sleep—not long—but long enough for him to slip inside her room. Where had Ben run off to? He'd said he was going to let the detective know she was ready to talk. His absence didn't explain how the Bishop had gotten in her room, or how he'd gotten past the guard at the door.

"Do we have an understanding?" the Bishop asked.

She didn't answer him so he gave her a little shake. "If you don't keep quiet and insist on telling the world about my son's *indiscretion* with you, then I'll take his *kinner* from you while you're in prison."

"Please," she squealed around his fingers, but the plea for mercy meant nothing to him. "Your *fraa* will tell what she saw; she knows I didn't push him. His fall was an accident, but he fell because he was trying to kill me."

His graying brows cinched over his angry eyes. "You're a liar! My *fraa* will tell the police what I tell her to; who do you think they'll believe? The word of the Bishop's *fraa*? Or the word of a jealous Jezebel who threw herself at my son one night and got exactly what she deserved?"

Eva continued to shake and whimper; where was the guard at her door and how had he gotten in here to talk to her?

She turned her head toward the door. "Guard!" she cried.

"It won't do you any good to call for him," he said, throwing his head back and laughing only for a moment. "I suspect that little fire I started in one of the empty rooms will have most of the staff busy just long enough."

She sobbed louder. "Help, help me!" she screamed.

His jaw clenched and his eyes narrowed, he clamped his hand back over her mouth. "If you make another sound," he said, holding a knife against her side. "I'll kill you both."

She let out a cry, curling her arms around her stomach to protect the baby. "Please don't hurt us; I'm sorry about what happened to Adam."

"You're not sorry, but I'm going to make you pay for his murder; an eye for an eye, the Bible says."

"No!" she screamed.

The door of her room burst open and the Bishop jumped back as the detective and two officers entered, guns trained on him.

"Drop the knife and put your hands up where I can see them," one of the officers said.

He dropped the knife and drew his hands upward in one smooth motion. One cuffed him while the other read him his rights. Had she heard the officer correctly? He was being charged with attempted murder—three counts.

Who was the third person?

Chapter Eighteen

Eva collapsed against her husband and sobbed. She'd cried so much her head ached.

"I'm sorry I wasn't here; we didn't think he'd come here and try to hurt you until we found *Frau* Byler half-dead near the road. We think she was trying to get help before she passed out in the grass. The officers almost didn't see her; she could have been run over by another car if we hadn't gone over there to get her statement. The Bishop had refused to let them talk to her, but they said they were going to see her anyway and I wanted to tag along."

"Did she say why he beat her up?"

Ben shook his head and sighed. "She hasn't regained consciousness and they aren't sure if she'll pull through."

"But she's my only witness!" Eva cried.

She hadn't meant for that to sound the way it had come out, she was desperate to prove her innocence. She'd even pleaded with the Bishop, telling him that she was sorry for what happened, hoping he'd understand that it was truly an accident.

Was she—sorry? Yes, she was, even though at one time she might have wished him dead for what he'd done to her. She didn't feel that way now; all she felt was guilt for her wrong thoughts.

She cleared her throat. "I'm sorry," she said to Ben. "I'm sure that must've sounded very selfish; I'll pray for her recovery but not for my sake."

The heavy burden weighing down her shoulders had suddenly lifted. A few hours ago, she had finally told the truth about Adam's violence against her, and now, she'd found out how good it was to get it all out in the open.

She lifted her head from Ben's shoulder. "Did you find my apron in the bathroom of the *dawdi haus*?"

He nodded. "The detective took both the items as evidence. He brought them to the morgue to be analyzed and compared to Adam's DNA. When I saw them, I—I'm so sorry about what he did to you, but hopefully that will help clear you of the murder charges against you. I think they'll still need to take a statement from Adam's mother. We need to pray that she'll pull through."

Eva glanced at the clock on the wall in the hospital room. "It's Christmas!" she said. "I wish I could be with Grace and give her the gift I made for her first Christmas."

Ben pulled away from her and smiled. "I didn't tell you the *gut* news; Emily invited my *mamm* and Grace to stay with her. Alma offered to bring them up here in the morning to see you."

Eva smiled. "I'm so happy she wants to spend time with her niece."

Ben put a finger under her chin, lifting it slightly and pressing his lips to hers. "I plan on staying right here with you and in the morning, I pray that we will have some news from those DNA results. I'd like to take you home where you belong."

Eva woke up when her nurse came in to check on her. Her gaze turned to her husband, who was sleeping in the chair next to the bed. She giggled inwardly as she listened to his light snoring. It was a sound she would love to get used to; she felt the safest in Ben's arms, but having him close was more than she could have ever hoped for.

The nurse went back out into the hall and brought a wheelchair with her. "Would you like to take a little ride?" She asked. "There is someone who would like to see you."

She looked over at Ben and hesitated. "What about the guard outside my door?"

The nurse nodded, a compassionate look across her face. "I suspect he'll tag along, but I think you'll be alright."

She looked back over at her husband, not wanting to disturb him, but at the same time, she did not want to be without his protection. She reached over and touched his arm lightly and waited for his lashes to flutter open. He focused on her and she smiled, giving his arm a little squeeze. He tucked his hand in hers, patting it with his other hand, his smile widening.

"Are we going somewhere?" he asked.

Eva nodded. "Would you like to go along?"

He yawned and stretched and then rose from the chair slowly and stretched again. "Let's go," he said.

The nurse grabbed the IV pouch hanging from the pole beside her bed and looped it onto the pole fixed to the wheelchair. Then, she unhooked the lead wires and turned off the monitor overhead. She assisted Eva into the wheelchair and placed a blanket over her lap. She wheeled her out into the hall where they were met with the new guard. They stopped at the elevator and Eva was a little confused. Surely, they would not take her down to the morgue and force her to view Adam's body.

She cleared her throat and looked behind her at the nurse. "Where exactly is it that we are going?"

The nurse smiled and winked. "It's a surprise," she said. "But I think you'll find it's a pleasant one."

Eva's heart rate slowed a little though her breathing didn't. Still a little nervous, she reasoned with herself that the woman would not smile and tell her it was a surprise if it was something very awful. Besides, the entire reason she was there was to keep her calm and lower her blood pressure. A shock such as viewing a dead body would probably give her a heart attack even in her young age.

The door swung open and the nurse wheeled her into the elevator. She looked up at the guard. "Sixth floor please," she said.

Eva breathed a sigh of relief; at least they weren't going to the basement where the morgue was. They rose to the sixth floor and Eva's stomach lurched.

The nurse wheeled her down the corridor and she glanced into each passing room until they stopped at room 605. The curtain was pulled around the bed but she could see The Amish dress and *kapp* in the chair at the end of the bed and knew she was there to visit with Adam's mother. Her heart sped up after the nurse pulled back the curtain, revealing a very battered and bruised woman. Her eyes were black and blue and swelled half way closed.

Several stitches held together an angled cut above her eye. Without meaning to, Eva gasped and pulled her hand quickly to her mouth, holding it there, her eyes wide.

The woman reached a hand out to her and Eva instinctively rose from the chair and took her hand. Her lower lip quivered and tears welled up in her eyes. What kind of a man would do such a thing to his own wife? He'd pledged to love her, provide for her, and protect her until death parted them. Sadly, there had been no one to save her from the one person who'd vowed to protect her.

Frau Byler looked up at the nurse and the guard. "Would you mind leaving Eva and her husband here with me so I can talk to them?"

Don't leave! Eva inwardly screamed. If this woman was about to confess the truth, she wanted more witnesses than just Ben.

Chapter Nineteen

Before Eva had a chance to protest, the nurse and the guard exited *Frau* Byler's room. Ben urged Eva back into the wheelchair, pushing her a little closer to the woman, who'd reached for her hand again.

"I wanted to tell you my story," the woman said with a weak voice.

It was hard for Eva to look at her without wanting to sob, but she bit her lip to keep her emotions in check.

Her foremost thoughts were that Adam's attacks on her could have been a lot worse—but what could be worse than being violated and forced into an unplanned pregnancy?

"When I was your age," Adam's mother said quietly, squinting to see Eva. "I met a very handsome *mann,* and I had stars in my eyes for him. He was sandy-haired and strong; he was *gut* with horses, and he could ride like he was born in the saddle. I was fascinated with him because he and his *familye* were new to the community, and the other boys seemed so dull compared to Henry. We hadn't grown up together so I had no idea what type of a *mann* he was in his heart. I only knew what I saw on the outside—that, and the polite gentleman that he showed to the world."

She paused, seemingly stuck in time.

"It didn't take long for him to show me his dark side—a side I was helpless to get away from. At first, his temper would flare out of control, but he never struck me. Then his friends introduced him to beer and wine; he began to drink heavily and he was mean when he was full of the liquid spirit. That's about the time he began to *hurt me*. He'd always apologize and promise it would never happen again. I foolishly trusted him and gave him too many chances; I truly wanted to fix things for him after he begged me to help him get away from the alcohol. But every time I tried, it made him angrier and more violent."

So far, the woman seemed to be describing her son rather than her husband. Was it possible that no one in the community was aware of the Bishop's problem with alcohol?

"I made excuses for him and believed him every time he said he was sorry—until the night he took things too far." She lowered her head and began to weep.

Ben handed her a tissue so she could go on; Eva was sickened by the story so far, but eager to get to the part where she confessed she'd lied to cover up for her son's wrongdoing and admit his death was an accident. It wasn't that she had no compassion for the woman; she truly did, but knowing her history wasn't going to change things—was it?

"One night, I'd decided I'd had enough of taking care of him and only getting slapped around for my efforts to help," she finally continued. "I met him at the covered bridge over Peace River—back when it was a working bridge. It was late at night and we had been running around because we were going to be married soon. I went to break it off with him, but he accused me of being a *tease,* and forced himself on me."

Eva's blood ran cold through her veins.

"I'd become pregnant with Adam that night; afterward, I did everything I could to avoid him. I fully intended never to see him again. When my *vadder* found out I was pregnant, he accused me of shaming the *familye* name and forced me to marry Henry so we wouldn't be shunned. I was afraid of him and didn't want to marry him, but my parents accused me of being promiscuous with Henry but that wasn't how it happened. I was young, and I didn't have the courage to speak up and tell them what he'd done. They blamed me and I've carried that shame with me all these years. When Adam was born, I distanced myself from him because he reminded me too much of his *vadder*. I even feared him growing up with the same evil inside him that Henry has—I was right in so many ways, but wrong in one very big way."

Eva leaned in toward her. "What were you wrong about?"

"I should have loved Adam more," she admitted, tears freely flowing from her swollen eyes. "I should have made sure he had some *gut* in him—from me, but instead, I allowed his *vadder* to raise him with his evil ways. I distanced myself from him because I didn't know how to love a child I didn't ask for."

Eva's heart sped up; she'd struggled with some of the same thoughts.

"Don't make the same mistake that I did," the woman urged her. "That child you carry didn't ask to come into the world the way it did, but each child is a child of *Gott,* and deserves to be loved—no matter who it's parents are. Shower that wee one with all the love you can give him—or her. Make sure that child *knows* that it's loved. Raise it right—with the word of *Gott,* and don't spoil the child. Discipline is important; teach the child right from wrong. I never taught Adam much of anything; I didn't have any kind of relationship with him. He watched his *vadder* hit me and listened to him mistreating me verbally, and somewhere along the way, he learned his ways. It was as if he didn't know any other way of treating women. He began to mistreat me a few years back, and he even hit me once recently. Since then, I knew he was destined to repeat his *vadder's* mistakes. I didn't have the courage to reach out to you before it was too late—I'm sorry for that."

Eva wept. "Adam did the same thing to me."

"I know," his mother said. "I overheard Adam mocking you and calling you the same dirty names his *vadder* called me the night he was conceived. When I overheard your argument with Adam last night, I had to accept that my son had become the same type of *mann* as his *vadder*. I wish I'd seen it before—before he fell to his death last night."

Eva's heart sank to her feet, adrenaline coating her mouth with a sticky dryness that made her cough.

"It seems that history repeated itself and both our children were conceived in the same place—and in the same way. I'm sorry for what my son did to you, and I promise you I will spend the rest of my life trying to make it up to you. I feel somewhat responsible because I know that if I'd taught him right from wrong, he might have turned out to be a *gut mann*. I have to believe that."

"I believe it," Eva said quietly. "He had potential. He wasn't always all bad. It was the drinking that changed him into what he was."

"That he learned from his *vadder* too," she said. "He gave him his first drink when he was only twelve—Henry told him it would make a *mann* out of him."

"I'm sorry about Adam," Eva said.

"I am too," his mother said. "I know his death was an accident, and that's why Henry beat me so badly this time—because I told him I was going to tell the truth about Adam."

"I'm sorry he treated you that way," Eva said.

"*Danki,*" *Frau* Byler said. "You might not agree with me but I've forgiven Henry for what he did; the police aren't happy with me that I won't press charges against him, but they said it would be up to the judge how long he'd stay in jail. He said he could get up to fifteen years, but without my testimony, I don't have any idea how long—just as long as he leaves me alone to live the rest of my life in peace. I've forgiven him, but I won't give him the chance to hurt me again."

"I don't blame you," Eva said. "I've done my share of forgiving too, and I think it's what's best—for us. I've even prayed for Adam's soul."

"I have too," his mother said. "but if you'll let me, I'd like another chance to make up for neglecting my own son by way of *his* child. I'd like to make sure it's raised with love, and never has to see the kind of violence that Adam saw when he was growing up."

"Danki," Eva said. "You're more than welcome to be a part of this child's life."

His mother wept; Eva rose from the wheelchair and leaned in to hug her, but hesitated, not wanting to hurt her.

The woman greeted her with outstretched arms. "Don't be afraid to hurt me; nothing can hurt me anymore now that Henry is locked away. I need to heal and to move on. I could really use a hug. I've spent almost my entire adult life without love and I have so much to give."

Eva could see what a big heart Adam's mother had. It wasn't fair that she'd been forced into a lifetime of suffering.

If Eva had anything to do with it, that was all about to change.

Chapter Twenty

Eva giggled at Grace's preoccupation with chasing after a butterfly in the garden. She tumbled into the grass, pouting at her failed attempt. She pointed at it, frustrated it wouldn't hold still so she could pluck it out of the air.

Eva leaned back on the quilt she'd spread out in the yard for the two of them. She wiped the sweat from her brow with the back of her hand, relieved she didn't have to chase after the very energetic Grace so late in her pregnancy. She could hardly move, let alone attempt to chase a precocious toddler who was just learning to walk.

"She's wearing me out!" Emily said, scooping up Grace in her arms and bringing her back to the large quilt. The screen door to the kitchen swung open with a squeak. Eva looked up and smiled when Emily jumped up from the quilt to help.

Frau Byler carried a tray of lemonade over to them, followed by her mother-in-law, who brought a tray of sandwiches.

Grace started to fuss and she reached out for the refreshment. "*Mammi* is bringing the lemonade, sweetie, hold on."

Frau Byler smiled at the term of endearment; she'd more than proved herself as a good grandmother for Grace for the past few months, which proved the woman would be more than ready to handle herself after her real grandchild was born. She and Emily had been staying with Eva while their houses were being sold in the other community. Eva hadn't blamed Adam's mother for wanting a fresh new start— away from the gossip of the community, where she could heal from her husband's disgrace.

With the two women there, Grace and the child she expected any day would be showered with the love of two grandmothers. Emily being there only added to it. Together, they could raise a happy, healthy child that would not follow in its father's footsteps.

Eva reached for the glass of lemonade and handed it to Grace; she nearly spilled it when another twinge in her back took her breath away. The pains had been coming regularly for several hours already, and that one nearly took her breath away.

"Where's Ben?" she asked the ladies.

"He should be coming up from the field any minute for the meal. Do you want me to ring the bell?"

Eva nodded, breathing through the very strong contraction.

Emily rang the dinner bell hanging from the porch post. It clanged in her head, but she was grateful it was loud enough that Ben would hear it if he was still in the field.

The pains had only been mere twinges when he'd gone out there hours ago after the morning milking, and so she hadn't bothered to say anything to him when he'd brought in the pail of milk for her.

Within minutes, Ben rode up on his horse; he'd taken him out there to drag away a fallen branch from the large oak tree in the center of the field. It had lost the branch in the summer storm last night.

He slid from the bare-back of the horse and looked toward Eva. "Is it time for dinner, or time for the *boppli?*"

"Both!" Eva said with a smile.

He started to walk toward her but looked at his hands, and his horse that needed tending to. "Do I have time to take care of Sugar and wash up first?"

Eva nodded, wincing at the pain that continued to peak until she let out a yelp.

His eyes widened with alarm. "That didn't sound like I have time to get you into the *haus.*"

She shooed him with her hand. "You've got time to do what you need to—but hurry, please."

Eva leaned back against the large maple tree and stretched her feet out to the edge of the quilt where the sun flickered on the wedding ring pattern his mother had sewn for them for a wedding gift.

Eva breathed through another contraction, this one more intense than the previous two put together. She'd barely had time to catch her breath from the last one before this one started.

"It won't be long now," Emily said to Grace. "And you'll be a big sister."

Eva hadn't given too much thought to how Grace would feel if she had to share her with a new baby. She'd been her baby since the first day she'd held her, and now she was going to have another one—and it would be no more her own than Grace was.

She remembered what Adam's mother had made her promise—to love the child—even if it looked like its father. Eva shook; was she ready to give birth to Adam's child? Would he know about it from beyond the grave? She prayed that he'd been repentant enough to make it to Heaven, but if he hadn't, she would do everything in her power to ensure his child's eternal life.

She'd long-since forgiven Adam for what he'd done, and truthfully, she already loved his child. It wasn't the child's fault, and she knew from raising Grace that the child she carried was a child of God.

Before she had another contraction, Ben was at her side. He lifted her from the quilt and carried her inside the main house. She'd asked Emily to assist with the birth since she was the closest to her. They'd mended fences shortly after Eva had left the hospital between

Christmas and the new year. It saddened her that she'd spent her wedding day and their first Christmas in the hospital after Adam's death, but they had more than made up for it. They had a lifetime of Christmases ahead of them, and a lot of love to share.

Ben helped Eva into her nightgown and made her comfortable on the bed. He propped up pillows behind her while Emily readied things for the baby's care after the birth.

A sudden, sharp contraction assaulted Eva and she grunted. "I have to push," she cried from the pain.

"Are you sure it's time?" Ben asked.

Her water broke just then and another contraction came at the tail end of the previous one, not giving her enough time to relax between the pains.

Emily brought towels to mop up the water, while Ben checked to see if the baby was crowning.

He smiled from the end of the bed. "It won't be long now; just blow out your breaths in short puffs. Don't hold your breath. On the next contraction, hold it in and push as hard as you can."

She did as her husband instructed and pushed until she felt the head emerging.

"Hold it for a minute so I can ease the head out."

"I hope you know what you're doing," she cried.

"I've birthed plenty of livestock," he said with a chuckle. "I even assisted Grace's birth, so if you trust me, I think we can do this."

She smiled briefly. "I trust you." He leaned up and kissed her just as the next contraction began. He eased out each shoulder and then the rest of the baby. He cleaned the mouth and suctioned the nose with a bulb syringe, and then tied off the cord, the baby wailing.

Eva giggled as Emily cleaned her and wrapped the baby in a blanket, and then put her in her arms. She stared at the infant, tears in her eyes, her heart swelling with love—instant love for the child.

The wee one wailed, but Eva began to coo to her. "I'm your *mamm,* and this is your *dat,*" she said turning the baby toward Ben. "You've got a big *schweschder* and an *aenti,* and two *grossmammi's* waiting to shower you with all the love you'll ever need. I prayed that *Gott* would give me a reason to live, and I had faith that you would be a little girl, and here you are. I prayed so long for you, and I had faith that you would be a little girl so Grace could have a *schweschder;* I think your name should be Faith—what do you think, Ben?"

He smiled, and reached for her. He kissed her forehead and held her close. "I'm going to have my hands full with two *dochders.* I think your *mamm* and I need to discuss a little *brudder* for the two of you or I'll be outnumbered in this *haus* with all you females."

Eva chortled. "I think we need to get the first two on their way first before we start thinking of adding another one."

He kissed Eva and smiled. "As long as the subject is open for discussion."

"Of course, it is." She loved the idea of giving him a son because she trusted that Ben would raise him to be a good man—just like him.

"Can we see the wee one yet?" Ben's mother called from the other side of the bedroom door.

"*Jah*," Eva said.

They all came in wanting to hold the baby, but it was Adam's mother who had earned first dibs. After all, she was the only blood relative besides Emily that the child would have.

She handed the baby to the anxious woman.

"Meet your new granddaughter, Faith."

Frau Byler smiled, tears welling up in her eyes. She reached for the child and pulled her close, kissing her little pink cheek. "I've been waiting for you my entire life," she said to Faith.

A knock at the front door interrupted her cooing, and she went to answer it, babe in her arms. She opened the door, unable to find her voice.

Bishop Byler stood there staring at her and the infant she held.

"Is that Adam's new *boppli*?"

Chapter Twenty-One

Melody Fisher hummed a hymn from the *Ausbund* as she steered her horse and buggy onto the new covered bridge over Peace Creek.

Chestnut's ears twitched as his hooves clapped down on the wooden planks and he let out a snort and a low groan.

An old man in a black hat unexpectedly stepped out from the shadows at the far end of the bridge, startling Melody.

She tightened up the reins, hoping he'd move, but he seemed as if he needed help.

He was Amish—Old Order, but she'd never seen him before. He was dirty, and his clothes were tattered—as if he was homeless; was such a thing possible in their community? Since she didn't know him, she didn't want to stop, but he was blocking the path and she couldn't go around him without hitting him.

"Whoa, Boy!" Melody said to Chestnut.

As the man approached, something in his eyes made her heart speed up. His stare made her nervous, and she darted her eyes to see if there was enough room to pass around him. He was on foot and could easily jump from one side to the next quickly and remain in her way. If she tried to back the horse, she'd hit the sidewall of the bridge.

Lily, her eight-year-old daughter, was at her shoulder from the back seat. "What's wrong, *Mamm?*"

"Sit back down, Lily," she said, trying to steady her shaky voice.

"Are you lost?" she called out to the old man, wondering where he'd come from since there wasn't an Old Order Amish community in the area.

He stopped near Chestnut, causing the animal to grunt and whinny, his ears twitching madly. The animal seemed to sense something was awry, and it made Melody so uneasy she could taste the stickiness of adrenaline on her tongue.

The old man narrowed his eyes. "I'm visiting *mei sohn.*"

"Where does your son live?" she asked.

He twisted up his face. "*Mei sohn* is dead!" he shouted.

Melody jumped.

She knew who he was; there were rumors in the community that the old Bishop had been let out of jail recently. But what would he be doing here at the bridge? Didn't he have an ankle bracelet on?

Her gaze traveled to his pant leg; just over his boot was a black band with two little boxes on each side of his leg, a green light blinking on one side.

"I went back to jail for another year because of you, when all I wanted to do was see *mei grandkinner.* Now I have to wear this ankle bracelet for another year!"

Melody shook her head; he had her mistaken for her cousin, Eva.

"When the police caught me at your house, they wouldn't listen to me; I only wanted to see *mei sohn's boppli,* and you wouldn't let me see her!"

Melody's breath hitched, and she lifted her gaze to meet his.

He chuckled. "I convinced them to extend *mei* boundaries to the bridge, so I could visit Adam, but I can't go beyond the bridge!" he said with a raised voice. "I've been waiting for you every day since I was set free. I told you I'd come back for you, Eva!"

Melody felt Lily at her back again, and she reached behind her to move the child back to her seat. "Eva's *mei* cousin," she said, her voice shaky.

She knew the history and the story behind this man's troubles, but she didn't look enough like Eva for him to mistake her for her cousin, did she?

"You're Eva Yoder and you killed *mei sohn!*"

Her flesh prickled as her blood ran through her veins with an icy chill.

"Nee," she cried, shaking her head. "I'm not Eva—it wasn't me!"

Melody tugged on the reins to back up the horse, but the Bishop grabbed the harness.

"You're not getting away, Eva, you're going to join Adam in the ravine."

Melody and Lily screamed.

Chestnut reared and squealed.

The Bishop waved his arms and hollered to agitate the horse, and then slapped his flank, causing him to buck.

Melody screamed, yanking on the reins and pulling back with all her might.

"Whoa!" She sobbed. "Stop it; leave me alone. I'm not Eva!"

From the back seat, Lily screamed as the open buggy jostled back and forth.

Melody convulsed with sobs as she snaked her hands around the reins hoping to control the horse. "Somebody help me!" she screamed.

The horse squealed and snorted as he lifted his front legs, causing the buggy to teeter, dumping Lily out onto the wooden floor of the bridge with a thud.

"Run, Lily, run home," Melody screamed.

261

Bishop Byler tightened his grip on the harnesses and shoved at the horse. He slapped his side so hard, he bolted backward about a hundred feet, slamming the buggy into the wall of the bridge. The sudden jolt threw Melody from her seat, catapulting her out the window head first. A fading scream escaped her on the way down the ravine until a small splash reverberated up from the shallow creek.

"Please help my *mamm*," Lily begged him. "Please!"

He rushed to the window and let out a belly laugh before turning to face Lily. "No one can help her now; she's joined *mei sohn* in the afterlife," he growled at her."

Lily stood in the middle of the bridge crying for her mother, her eyes wide and fearful, but she couldn't move.

As the Bishop ambled toward her, Lily's breaths came in short bursts, propelled only by the uncontrollable sobbing that now shook her limbs. Tears slid down her cheeks and her nose dripped. She stood there not moving until the Bishop was almost too close to run from.

He took another step toward her, as if it was a game to him. Lily inched back toward the end of the bridge after he took another step. Her whole body shook, and she heaved in her breaths. The Bishop quickened his steps, closing the space between them. Her eyes locked with his and she blinked away tears.

She stumbled as her foot teetered over the threshold of the bridge into the dirt road. She fell backward, bracing herself with her hands.

The Bishop reached the edge of the bridge and bent down to grab her, but she scooted backward on her haunches. His hand caught the end of her shoe; she screamed as she wriggled out of it and scrambled backward in the dirt.

Her gaze dropped when the blinking green light on his ankle bracelet turned red. The Bishop looked down at his ankle and then stood there staring at her as he drew back his leg. The device blinked green again.

I can't go beyond the bridge, he'd told her mother.

Bishop Byler lurched forward, grabbing for her once more, catching the end of her foot, but she pulled on it and scooted back out of his reach.

He stopped and stared at her for a minute; she was still sobbing, but content that he couldn't leave the bridge; his ankle bracelet would alert the police and he'd go back to jail.

Lily watched him, fear paralyzing her.

"We'll meet again," he said with a slight chuckle. "I promise!"

She sat there in the dirt, unable to move, as she watched him walk back toward the other end of the bridge and out of sight.

Chapter Twenty-Two

Lily stared with unseeing eyes while Chestnut bucked repeatedly, his whinnying muffled. The sun sparkled over Peace Creek, the reflection nearly blinding her.

Her *mamm* was down there somewhere below the bridge; she needed help, but Lily hadn't moved. How long she'd sat there was unknown to her.

Chestnut bucked again, startling her.

Her gaze lifted to the struggling animal, but she couldn't help him; she needed to help her *mudder.*

Pushing herself up from the ground, her limbs were shaky and caused her to stumble back into the dirt. She tried a second time and lost her footing again. Fresh sobs shook her tiny frame as she attempted a third time to rise to her feet, but it was no use; she was too weak and shaky.

She rose to her knees and scrambled across the dirt road into the grassy area that led down a steep embankment to the creek below.

She peered over the edge of the drop and let out a strangled cry. Her *mamm* was down there, half in the water.

"*Mamm,*" she screamed, sobs convulsing her when she didn't get a response.

Turning around, she slowly skidded down feet first, grappling the tall, grassy plants for leverage.

About mid-way, she looked down at her mother; panic seized her, paralyzing her momentarily.

"I can't save you, *Mamm,*" she blubbered. "I'm sorry!"

She leaned forward in the grass and pressed her face against it, hugging the steep levee of warm earth. Shifting slightly, her foot slipped on a rock, sending her tumbling down head over heels several times in between screams.

Landing upright on a ledge, she looked down at her mother; her head was spinning, and she closed her eyes to keep from vomiting. She didn't have much further to go, but it was a steep grade. Her gaze traveled to the edge of the grassy shelf where she'd landed, locating a spot where she could jump to the next ridge; it was mostly level ground from that point to where her mother lay face-up on the creek bank.

"I'm coming, *Mamm,*" Lily cried out.

Her voice echoed in the gully.

She looked up toward the bridge where she could hear Chestnut still whinnying and snorting about his displeasure with being jammed up against the side of the bridge.

She shimmied over to the end of the low rise she'd settled onto and turned back around to inch her way down the rest of the way into the ravine to rescue her mother. She shook and sobbed, which made her journey more difficult, but fear for her mother pushed her forward.

When she was close enough to see her mother clearly, she was elated to see that her eyes were open. "*Mamm,* I'm coming," she called down to her.

Picking up her pace, she slipped several times in the tall grass that was still damp from early morning dew. Her hands and knees were scraped and bloody, but she pressed on, determined to reach her mother.

"*Mamm,* I'm here," Lily said, collapsing beside her mother.

Melody winced when her daughter laid her head on her chest, and as much as she wanted Lily near, she feared for her safety with the Bishop still in the area.

"How...did you...get away?" Melody asked, coughing. "Where... is he?"

Lily shook her head. "He's gone; I don't know where he went."

Melody struggled to breathe; she'd known for several minutes that she could not move even her fingers. She cried out asking for safety for Lily and she was here with her now. Though she did not want to be alone because she sensed she was dying, she needed to be sure Lily was safe.

"Go... home," she said. "I don't...want him... to hurt... you." She coughed weakly.

Lily shook her head vigorously, sobs consuming her. "No, *Mamm;* I won't leave you."

"Tell…your…*Dat* what…happened."

Lily wiped tears that dripped down the side of Melody's face, shushing her mother in between sobs.

Melody coughed again and felt something trickle down the side of her face.

Lily's eyes bulged. "*Mamm,* you're bleeding. Let me help you up; you have to see the doctor."

Melody's eyes filled with fresh tears; she knew she could not move, let alone, try to walk away from this accident. "*Nee,* I'm going…to be with…*Gott.* I can't…go with you."

"*Nee,* please don't leave me," Lily begged her.

Melody coughed harder, her breath hitching. "I...love…you."

"I love you too, *Mamm,*" Lily said, dropping her head to her mother's chest, sobbing even harder.

Melody breathed in the sweet smell of honeysuckle in her daughter's hair just before everything went black.

Chapter Twenty-Three

Lily held her mother long after her heart stopped beating. She'd stopped sobbing, except for the occasional hitch in her breath, hoping to hear her mother's heartbeat once more. The sun was high overhead and it burned her skin, but she would not leave her mother's side.

Above her, on the bridge, clip-clop of horse's hooves clattered across the bridge. Lily's heart sped up; was the bad man with the black hat coming back to hurt her?

"Hello," a voice called out.

Did she know that voice? It was almost muffled, as if she was under water. She lifted her ear from her mother's heart and looked toward the bridge. The sun blinded her view of the person standing in the cutout window of the bridge.

"Lily," the voice called. "Melody—are you alright? Stay there, I'm coming down there."

"It's *Dat;* he's going to help you," Lily whispered.

She sucked in a breath and let it out with a burst of tears. Her father would make it right; he'd take her mother to the doctor and she would be alright.

Hurry, Dat.

She laid her head back down on her mother's chest and listened for her heart.

"Please come back," she cried. "*Dat* is coming and he'll help you."

She sobbed harder; she knew her mother wasn't coming back to her.

She knew.

Sam Fisher rushed down the ravine to get to his wife and daughter, slipping several times on the uneven terrain. How had they gotten down there? Every few feet, he looked down at them, and judging by his daughter's crying, something was seriously wrong.

"Melody," he called out to his wife.

Why wouldn't she answer him?

His heart beat hard against his chest wall, his breathing labored, as he made his way closer to them. Lily rested on her haunches, hovering over her mother and sobbing. Fear gripped him when he realized she could be severely hurt—or worse.

"Hurry, she needs you!" Lily cried out.

Sam looked up; he'd made it more than halfway down, but the worst rocky part was still between him and his family.

"Hang in there, Lily," he said, bending to brace his hands against the rocks to help him down. "How's your *mamm?*"

"She's bleeding," Lily called up to him. "She won't move."

Bleeding?

Won't move?

Had she fallen from the bridge? Judging from the way the buggy was wedged into the side of the bridge and where she lay on the ground—half in the creek, he imagined the worst.

Gott, give me the strength to face this trial.

With his back to his daughter, her crying became louder every step he took to reach her. He turned several times, nearly losing his footing, but the scene at the bottom of the creek bed was the same.

When he finally reached a spot where he could stand upright without grappling onto the grass and rocks, he hesitated before resuming his journey. He already knew his wife was dead; he could feel it in his soul. He bit back tears, knowing that to fall apart in front of Lily would not be good for her.

He would be strong—for Lily.

Before he reached his wife and daughter, someone from the bridge called out to him—an *Englisher.* "Do you need help?" the man asked, holding up his phone.

Sam stopped and nodded up toward the man, knowing he would need help getting his family back up the side of the ravine. "*Jah.*"

Then he collapsed next to his daughter, pulled her sobbing, shaky frame into one arm, and grabbed his wife's wrist with his other hand. He moved his fingers around in a panic; there was no pulse. Moving Lily over, he laid his head on Melody's chest to listen for her heartbeat.

He didn't find one.

His breath hitched, but he bit down hard on his cheek to keep his emotions in check; right now, his daughter needed him, and there was nothing to do for his beloved wife.

He picked up Lily, but she grappled onto her mother's light blue dress, clenching with iron fists.

"Let me stay with *Mamm,*" she screamed. "I have to protect her."

The more he tried to pull her away, the louder she screamed; it broke his heart.

He let her go and held her in one arm, and picked up his wife's hand, pulling it close to his cheek. Sobs caught in his throat, but he let them go; he just couldn't hold it in any longer.

It wasn't long before sirens reached his ears. Sam dried his face and wiped his nose on the sleeve of the blue, button-down shirt Melody had sewn for him. She'd always gotten after him for that; she'd pushed a handkerchief in the pocket of his broadfall pants every day hoping to tame his bad habit. He reached into his pocket, but there was no hanky; she must have forgotten today. She'd left the *haus* early to deliver fresh eggs to their neighbors, so they would have them for their Sunday morning meal before church service.

Why hadn't he stopped her? She'd pecked his lips with a quick kiss and then drove off with a smile and wave.

A rescue team was already lowering a rescue gurney from the side of the bridge with a wince, and paramedics were upon them. How had they gotten down the bottom of the ravine so quickly? Their voices were muffled in Sam's ears, and they prodded him with questions he couldn't comprehend.

When they tried moving Lily aside, she belted out a primal scream.

Sam snapped back to reality and scooped up his kicking and screaming daughter, pulling her away from her mother so the paramedics could put her on the stretcher.

They examined her body, shaking their heads, the hopeless looks on their faces stabbing at Sam's heart.

He held Lily tightly, so they could strap his wife to the blue, plastic stretcher, then they connected it to the cable and raised it up to the bridge. He turned Lily away so she wouldn't see what was happening to her mother, but she was so out-of-control, he could barely hold onto her. It frightened him that she could be so stricken with grief; he'd never seen her act out like this before.

A police officer approached him. "It looks like your horse must have been spooked—probably by a snake. By the looks of your buggy and the angle it's tipped backward, I'd say your wife was thrown clear from the seat and out the window. She appears to have died on impact, so I don't believe she suffered. I'm sorry for your loss." His voice was loud, and he spoke in choppy sentences in between Lily's cries.

Sam nodded mindlessly. At least she didn't suffer; he wished he could say the same for his daughter.

"After we get the pictures we need of the scene, we'll help you to get the buggy unhooked from the railing on the bridge; hopefully, then your horse will calm down. He's pretty agitated."

Again, Sam nodded; there was nothing he could do or say to bring back his wife, and nothing that would calm his child or his own aching heart.

Chapter Twenty-Four

Sam stood near his wife's grave, Lily at his side. She whimpered quietly while the Bishop spoke the eulogy. She hadn't spoken once in the past three days, and she'd barely eaten anything.

News of Melody's accident had made the front page of the newspaper, and plenty of *English* folks had come to the funeral to pay their respects.

Sam stared at the flowers that lay on Melody's casket; he'd picked them from her garden. In only one season, she'd planted a whole lifetime of flowers, nurturing the seedlings until they'd bloomed fully. She'd brought most of the clippings from the rose bushes from her own garden after the landlord had decided he no longer wanted to rent to them. With no parents to bequeath them property, they'd always rented, and Sam had finally earned enough to pay for a small mortgage. Being a harness maker wasn't the most profitable, but he'd used his skills to sell bridles to the western store in town, and that had made up the difference.

Now, he had no reason to build the house they'd dreamed about for so many years.

Lily clung to his side; what was he going to do with her? Melody had left him with no instructions. Even if she could have, he was still lost—especially since she hadn't spoken to him once since he allowed the paramedics to remove her mother's body from the ravine.

It had seemed like months had passed since that day; perhaps they were both still in shock from it, but he didn't know how he was going to function without her. Melody's cousin, Emily, had offered to come and help for a while, and he'd agreed, though he hadn't figured out how that was going to work out. He only prayed it would not be awkward being a guest in her own home; she'd been their landlord for the past year, and she'd been a good one, but this was different.

She was his wife's family—not his.

Would the Bishop approve of such an arrangement? Emily was a single woman, and now, he was a widower. Perhaps he should have checked with him first.

As the Bishop ended the funeral, the pallbearers began to lower Melody's casket into the ground. Sam felt Lily slip away from his side; her ear-piercing scream startled him, bringing his gaze in focus.

"Don't take her away from me!" Lily cried.

Lily had been to other funerals in the community; she knew enough about death to accept the routine of a funeral, didn't she?

Sam snapped out of his own thoughts and scooped up Lily the same way he'd had to at the edge of Peace Creek. Only now, the entire community and more was there to witness his child's breakdown. He wished he could spare her the hurt he, himself, was feeling, but there did not seem to be any reasoning with her.

He held her close and told her it was going to be alright.

"*Nee,*" she cried. "I need to tell her I'm sorry."

Sam's heart slammed against his ribcage, a million thoughts crowding his mind.

"What are you sorry for?" he asked in her ear. "This wasn't your fault."

It was a random accident and probably not preventable—unless she'd stayed home that morning. But that just wasn't in Melody's nature; she was always thinking of others above herself. She would only have stayed home that morning if he'd asked her to.

If anyone was to blame, it was him; he'd been too busy to hitch up the horse that morning, and Melody was too good-natured to pull him away from his work to ask for help. Perhaps if he'd helped her, the timing might have been different, and the horse might not have encountered whatever it was that had spooked him that morning.

"She told me to run and I didn't listen to her." Lily sobbed. "I should have run home and told you to help her. She told me to and I didn't mind her."

Sam pulled his daughter away from his shoulder to look into her eyes. "What are you talking about?"

"He killed her, and I didn't run to you for help."

"Chestnut didn't mean to hurt your *mamm,*" he said.

"Chestnut was scared," Lily said. "He scared him."

"Who?" Sam asked. "Who scared Chestnut?"

"I don't know his name." she cried. "*Mamm* told me to run and I didn't run. I'm sorry."

"What did he look like?"

"I'm sorry," she repeated.

"Was there someone there that day on the bridge?" Sam asked his daughter.

Lily screamed and buried her head in her father's shoulder.

"Tell me, Lily," he begged. "Did someone see what happened to your *mamm?*"

Lily lifted her head, her eyes glazed over with a fear he'd never seen in her.

"Red light—green light," she said.

"What are you talking about?"

"Green light—red light—green light."

Lily wouldn't stop repeating the phrase no matter how much he tried to reason with her. She said it loudly at first, until it turned into mumbles that were almost inaudible.

Sam carried her away from the funeral and back to the waiting buggy, patting Chestnut on the head before putting his delirious daughter in the back seat.

Chapter Twenty-Five

Emily Yoder steered Molasses up to the new bridge that stretched across Peace Creek and pulled back suddenly on the reins.

"Whoa, Boy!"

The horse stopped with a jolt, causing her small buggy to wobble. Perhaps she'd pulled a little too hard, but her shaky hands couldn't be stilled.

The hair on the back of her neck stood on end. Could she cross this same bridge that had taken the life of her cousin, Melody? She feared this bridge for more reasons than her cousin's death. They'd ruled Melody's death as a freak accident, calling it the fault of the horse. Something had spooked that horse; Adam's ghost, perhaps? She didn't believe in all that stuff, but there was a lot of hushed talk in the community about it—especially after Lily's breakdown. She'd claimed there was a man who'd spooked the horse—not in so many words, but it was the conclusion.

She drew in a deep breath, hoping to calm her foolish thoughts.

Her heart raced at the thought of crossing the bridge, and she held her breath with a long gasp. It wasn't the same bridge that had claimed Adam's life, but it still crossed Dead Man's Ravine over the very spot where he'd fallen to his death a year ago. Now, with Melody's death on the new bridge only a few days ago, the community was in a state of unrest.

She couldn't help but remember that night on the old bridge when Adam had tried to harm her and her twin sister, Eva. Though more than a year had passed, she could still hear the echo of Adam's scream as if it hung over the ravine like a thick fog; it haunted her.

She shivered from the early morning chill in the air; could she cross the new covered bridge? Immediately after Adam's accidental fall last year, the city had gone to work tearing down the narrow, one-lane bridge, and had constructed a wider bridge in its place. No, it wasn't the same bridge; it didn't even look the same. But since her cousin had fallen to her death, the ravine had claimed the lives of two people she knew.

Unfortunate for her, she needed to cross the bridge in order to reach her destination: her childhood home.

It was too late to go around the other way; Sam was expecting her.

Molasses whinnied and snorted, and bobbed his head up and down. Emily's heart drummed against her ribcage as she pulled the slack in the reins. "Whoa, Boy!" she called to him with a shaky voice.

Something had spooked him.

Gooseflesh tingled up her arms and ruffled the hair at the back of her neck.

She kept a tight hold of the reins.

Though the horse wasn't anxious to get across the bridge; she was. The horse had no real worries or bad memories of nearly being killed in this very spot. She'd been lucky that night that the same thing that had happened to her twin sister, Eva, had not happened to her.

So why was he so spooked? Was it the same thing that had spooked Melody's horse last week?

She'd attended the funeral in town at the cemetery yesterday, and that was the closest she'd come to this area of the community for a year. She'd been too shaken up to come back.

Cousin Alma had rented out Emily's childhood home to their cousin, Melody, and her family. Now that Melody's daughter was without a mother, she had agreed to take over her care. To do that, she needed to return to her home.

After what had happened on the bridge that night with Adam, she'd packed her things and left her home in the community to stay with Alma. Then, when Eva was near the end of her pregnancy, she stayed with her until she was back on her feet after the birth. She couldn't keep running from the past—and she couldn't let the random accident that happened to her cousin paralyze her.

I'm alright; I'm just spooked—like Molasses. I'm sure it's nothing.

The pep-talk she was giving herself wasn't making her limbs stop shaking. She had a bad feeling, but she had to get across the bridge. If she went around the long way, it would take her another thirty minutes, and she was already late. She'd promised to meet Sam, her cousin's widow, to go over everything she needed to know so she could keep Lily's routines as familiar as possible. The poor child had suffered a breakdown after seeing her mother thrown from the buggy and hadn't spoken a sensible word since.

At the funeral, she'd stared blankly the entire service, until they went to lower the casket into the grave. She'd screamed and thrown herself over the coffin and wouldn't let go until she was nearly passed out with exhaustion. The doctor had needed to sedate her to keep her from repeating the strange phrase that no one could figure out.

Emily shuddered just remembering what a scene the child had made, but truthfully, she'd wanted to do the same thing when her own mother had died. She hadn't been ready to let her go any more than she was ready to let her father go. She knew exactly how Lily felt, but the difference was, Lily was only a child; Emily's losses were more recent.

Was she prepared to handle such a troubled child?

Even if she wasn't, Lily was family, and for that reason, she would do all she could to help.

Emily rubbed her arms and hugged herself; could she allow Molasses to drive across the bridge while she kept her eyes closed? No; if he'd been on the bridge before she would trust him more, but this bridge was just as unfamiliar to him as it was to her.

Her gaze traveled the length of it; they'd made it somehow longer than the old bridge; it would take her a little longer to get across. She eyed the open window cutouts; it was rumored the city planned to enclose the openings with bars to prevent any more falls. A lot of good that would do her now; her buggy was just as open as Melody's, and her horse was more spirited than Chestnut. Naming her horse Molasses had been a joke; he did like to run when he wasn't supposed to.

Her first thought was to jump down and walk Molasses across; it was the only way she was going to get across, because she had no intention of dying today. If anyone should see her, would they think she was a fool, or would they understand?

Oh, what did she care for? It was her life! She was burning daylight sitting here trying to decide.

She hopped down from the buggy and grabbed onto the lead straps. She patted her horse on the side and set him at a slow walk. It was silly, and in her mind, she calculated how long it would take her to go around whenever she needed to go this direction, knowing it was necessary to visit Eva and her growing family. She supposed she'd have to cross it again when the opportunity presented itself, and perhaps, in time, she'd become more used to it. Today, she would walk, and her heart wouldn't beat normally again once the short journey ended.

Reconsidering her offer as a temporary nanny for eight-year-old Lily, Emily steered Molasses into the yard of her childhood home. It had been a long year since she'd rented the home out to the Fishers. It was only natural that she rent to Melody and her husband; it was best to keep her farm in the family until she was ready to live there again. Melody's death had made that decision for her. The strange accident had forced her to decide sooner than she'd planned, but sometimes it's best not to let old worries linger too long.

Naturally, Emily had offered her services as a caretaker at the funeral, and now she wondered if that was the best decision she could have made. She hadn't thought about how strange it would be to move back into her home until she sat here now staring at it.

If she'd known it would feel this foreign to her, she'd have backed out of her offer. She sighed heavily; going back on her word was not an option.

She climbed down from her buggy, wondering if Sam was in the house or the barn. Her gaze followed the trim yard and the newly-painted porch; Sam had done a lot of work to clean the place up. At the back side of the house, her mother's garden took her breath away.

A white, picket fence enclosed flowering plants and rose bushes in the most vibrant colors she'd ever seen. Butterflies fluttered above the plants, alighting on the colorful blossoms. A smile curved her lips; she knew her cousin kept a beautiful flower garden, but she never dreamed she'd plant such a beautiful garden out of the dead mess she'd left behind when she'd moved to the city with Alma.

Her gaze followed the trail of color until she noticed Lily standing among the plants. Her deep purple dress blended with the flowers and she almost didn't see her.

"Lily," she called out to her, but the girl did not turn around.

"Lily," she called again.

The child turned around and stared at her blankly. When Emily took a step toward her, Lily screamed and ran into the garden, hidden among the maze of plants.

Emily lifted her eyes and sighed.

Lord, give me strength; this isn't going to be easy.

Chapter Twenty-Six

Emily followed Sam around her old house as he instructed her and *showed her around;* she humored him, knowing he wasn't in the best state of mind, and had probably forgotten that this was her house up until a year ago when he and Melody had moved in.

"I'm sorry about Lily," he said. "She and Melody spent the entire summer in that garden; I suppose she feels closest to her there. She won't let anyone in there—not even me!"

Emily felt helpless to save her cousin's child from the grief she likely didn't understand. "I'm sure in time…"

Sam nodded. "Well, I'm sure you don't need me to tell you how to run a *haus*— especially not this one. You already know where everything is. I'm sorry if I'm rambling, but this is awkward for me. You and I don't really know each other, but I know Melody would have trusted you to fill in for her with Lily in her absence."

He turned away from her and cleared his throat.

Emily felt sorry for him; it couldn't have been easy for him to say that, but she really appreciated it.

"Danki," she said.

She resisted the urge to place a comforting hand on his shoulder; he was only a couple of years older than she was, and a very handsome man at that. She did not want him getting the wrong idea. She would save her comforting for Lily—if she would let Emily get anywhere near her, that is.

He coughed and cleared his throat again before facing her. "I know it's late, but I couldn't get Lily to eat anything; perhaps you could fix her a little snack and leave it on the table near the garden. They used to have tea and cookies out there."

She held a hand up to stop him; he was getting too choked up and she didn't want him torturing himself like that. Melody had been a lucky woman to have a man love her that way. She didn't think she'd ever get a chance to marry; Adam had been her only hope, and that had not ended well for her. The only good thing that had come from Adam was her niece, Faith.

Eva had gotten lucky with Ben; would marrying a widower be her only hope for marriage too? She shook the thought from her head; she was not there to marry Sam, she was there to take care of her cousin's daughter. Shame on her for letting her mind wander to such prideful thoughts.

"I'm afraid my only experience is with my sister, Eva's, toddlers," Emily offered, hoping it would change the subject enough to calm his worries.

"My Lily is acting like one for the past few days, so that might make it easier for you to handle her," he said quietly. "I want you to take care of her as if she was your own *kinner;* she doesn't have a *mamm* anymore, so she'll need one."

How long was Sam planning on having her stay; until Lily was grown up? She'd be a spinster by then. Surely, he didn't mean for her to raise her cousin's daughter. He was grieving, so she would not try to read anything into his words.

A knock at the door interrupted the awkward silence between them, and Emily was grateful. Donning an apron, she set to work on a snack for her and Lily while Sam went to the front door to answer it. Low voices made their way to the kitchen; it was the newly-appointed Bishop Yoder, whom Emily had not yet met.

He'd taken Bishop Byler's place after he'd gone to jail last year.

Sam brought him into the kitchen and introduced him. He seemed like a pleasant sort of man, but he seemed troubled about something.

"Melody was your cousin?" he asked a bit sternly.

She nodded. "*Jah.*"

"So, then you're not related to Samuel?"

She shook her head.

What was with all the questions; she had a child to care for and didn't have time to answer the same questions reworded.

"You're here to care for the wee one?"

She busied herself after nodding again, hoping he would get the message.

"Where will you be staying?"

She knew now what he was getting at. Sam had offered to move his things out of the main house and stay in the *dawdi haus* so she would be there for Lily. She knew the rules about having an escort for such an extended stay.

Sam spoke up and relayed the sleeping arrangements.

He shook his head. "*Nee,* that isn't *gut* enough," he said. "I understand this is legally your home, but you cannot stay on the same property with a widower, especially since you're an unmarried woman."

Emily bit back the urge to talk back to the Bishop; she would let Sam handle it. They were men and she need not put herself in the position to make herself look bad on a first meeting with the new Bishop.

"I'm afraid your community standing is already under review after Lily's behavior at Melody's funeral service," he said sternly. "When it comes up that you have willingly entered into such an agreement with regard to your living arrangement, I'm afraid I have no choice but to insist you must marry. Otherwise, you cannot reside on the same property. You know the rules—both of you."

Sam pursed his lips. "The grass has not even grown over Melody's grave and you're talking marriage to me?"

Emily felt her heart thump; she was mourning for her cousin, but not nearly in the same way Sam must be. She could not marry her husband; it would feel like a betrayal.

Surely, Sam would agree with that.

"Don't think of it in that way," the Bishop said. "It must be a marriage of convenience—for the sake of your *dochder*. She needs a *mudder*."

"*Jah,* I agree," Sam said.

What?! How can you agree with the Bishop? He's wrong!

"You can still take your mourning period," the Bishop said. "You can even stay out in the *dawdi haus* the way you'd planned, but in the eyes of the community, you've done the right thing and married her to take care of your *dochder.*"

Emily didn't dare turn around; they were talking about her as if she was not even there—and as if she had no say-so on the matter. It was not fair to any of them to agree to such an arrangement in order for Lily to be taken care of.

Sam was not answering the Bishop; Emily could feel the heat rising in her cheeks.

"I can marry you both now since you've taken the baptism, and we can keep it quiet until I can make an announcement at the services tomorrow," he said. "At that time, I will announce the marriage to the community to avoid giving anyone the chance to start any rumors."

Still no answer from Sam.

"I know this is a tough decision, but I'm sure you'll agree it's the only one to be made under the circumstances. You know if the situation were reversed, I'd be here advising the same thing to your widow."

What a harsh and cold thing to say!

Emily was fuming; she wanted Sam to make him leave, to tell him that community standing was not as important as healing from such a loss as he'd suffered.

And what of Lily? Doesn't she have a say in getting a new *mamm?* Emily hadn't even had the chance to get too near her without her getting spooked and running from her; how was she going to react when she finds out her mother has been replaced so quickly?

Emily couldn't quiet her mind; she was tempted to speak all of it to the Bishop, but it wasn't her place. It was Sam's—so why was he not speaking up?

The Bishop sighed at Sam's hesitation.

"If you don't marry Emily, she'll have to leave at once, and you'll have no one to care for Lily."

"Jah, I'll marry her," Sam said with a sigh.

What? Don't I get a say-so?

It took every bit of strength Emily had in her not to turn around and leave the house, but she had to remember she was there for Lily—not for Sam!

Chapter Twenty-Seven

He'd pressed a brief kiss to her cheek and thanked her for agreeing to marry him! Never had she thought she would be thanked at her wedding by her groom; it wasn't every girl's idea of a dream wedding. She couldn't change the facts; she was married—in name only.

Her cheek was still warm where he'd kissed her, and that bothered her just a little bit.

Her heart fluttered around in her chest as if it was trying to beat, but it was lost in emotion—emotions Emily could not put a name to. If she had to guess, she'd call it shame, or embarrassment, or perhaps regret.

She was stuck! This was it—until death parted them.

There hadn't been time to change her clothes or to talk to Eva or Alma first. More than that—there hadn't been time to change her mind.

She'd said a brief prayer, but her mind was too cluttered to know if God had answered her or not, and she might have mistaken Sam's willingness as God's will.

What had she done?

The bishop had left as swiftly as he'd whirled in, and Sam was back out in the barn working as if nothing had happened. She bit back tears; it was her wedding day—a wedding without love.

She was thankful Lily had not interrupted their impromptu kitchen-wedding ceremony. If she could call it that. He'd avoided all the sentimental words and gotten right to the vows; it had not lasted more than three minutes, and it was over.

She was married!

She leaned over the sink and tried to calm the queasiness in her stomach. Eva had married for convenience, but she'd had the time to grow her love for Ben first. Albeit, they hadn't had long together first, but surely longer than the time she'd been in Sam's company. She hadn't been there more than an hour before the Bishop was demanding they make a lifetime commitment to one another.

Oh no! Was she about to be sick?

Was she being punished by God, Himself, for thinking Sam was a handsome widower?

Ach, Lord, forgive me. If we've acted in haste, please help us to find a way to make it work. Put love in my heart for that mann, and soften his heart toward me, even if he can never love me. I can live with him if he's a gentle mann...Lord, help me to calm down and come to terms with this. And bless Lily so she can accept it. Help me not to think selfish thoughts.

It was tough not to think selfish thoughts; she was, after all married, and had lost the stigma of dying a spinster. She was also a mother—something she never thought she would be. She'd always dreamed of it, but never dared to hope for such a thing to avoid being disappointed in her life. The likelihood of her having her own child was not very high, but she'd make Melody proud and be the best mother she could be to Lily.

Speaking of Lily; she took in a deep breath and blew it out slowly, and then went about the task of cutting up a fresh apple, thinking some berries would be nice to make some tarts. She knew Melody was famous for her berry tarts, and she had a feeling she may be able to win a little favor with Lily if she made her some. Her cousin had taught her how to make them, teasing her recently at Eva's house that they would help her to get a husband; if she only knew Emily was thinking of making some for *her* family, she might be unhappy with her.

Was such a thing possible? Would Melody look down from Heaven and be unhappy with her? Or was Heaven truly as grand as the Bible says, and she would be too happy walking streets paved with gold and living in the presence of God to pay any attention to the things that worry a woman here on earth?

She shook away her foolish thoughts; Sam would never be a real husband to her. The best she could hope for would be that the other women in the community would not spread rumors about her fake marriage.

No woman likes to be married out of obligation; it would pour salt in the wound if the women in the community suspected there was no hope for a real marriage between them. It was bad enough she thought it herself. She would be the perfect Amish *fraa* for Sam and the perfect *mamm* to Lily.

The kitchen door burst open and it startled Emily.

"*Mamm,*" Lily said, staring blankly. "I need you! Come quick!"

Had Sam told her about them getting married? Surely, Lily wouldn't call her *Mamm* already.

"What do you need, Lily?" Emily asked.

Lily turned her head, paused, and then squealed. Then, she ran out the door, sobbing as if she'd just remembered her mother was gone.

Emily put a hand over her heart, her breath catching in her throat. That child was going to take five years off her life every time she saw her if she didn't find a way to break her of the screaming habit. Sam had told her that it was new since the accident, and he'd even said she'd done the same thing to him, so she tried not to take it personally, and remember she was just a child.

She took another deep breath and finished preparing the snack that she prayed Lily would eat.

Chapter Twenty-Eight

Emily readied herself for church early, so she could cook a proper breakfast; she would have to cook in her apron to keep her plain dress from getting dirty. Last night's dinner had been a disaster; luckily, there was still plenty of casseroles left over from the funeral and she hadn't had to make too much effort.

Getting Lily to sit at the table had been another story; Sam had reprimanded her more than once to sit still and eat after she pushed her food around her plate so much it ended up all over the table, and then when she shoved her plate and spilled her milk—that had been the last straw for poor Sam's nerves, and it was the end of Emily's good dress. With milk down the front of her church dress, she'd washed it and hung it up, hoping it would dry by morning, but it hadn't. She'd had to put on a work dress to wear to the service.

After making his daughter leave the table to go to her room, she'd fallen asleep in her clothes and without a bath. Emily laid awake most of the night in her childhood bedroom praying that the whole idea of her being here hadn't been a mistake. It was too late for wondering; she was married, and like it or not, she was now Lily's mother.

This morning, Lily resisted every effort Emily made to get her ready, but she was persistent. She'd run a bath for her and set out her clothes; she'd done everything short of putting Lily in the bathtub—in her nightgown, but that was next if she didn't mind. She'd been raised with discipline, and by the way Sam had handled her last night over the dinner fiasco, she was certain he would not object to her being strict with her parenting measures.

He'd told her to treat Lily as if she was her mother, and tossing her in the tub in her nightgown was certainly something Melody would do with her unruly child.

What she couldn't figure out about Lily was why she was acting up toward her—they'd always gotten along so well at family functions. She would probably understand it more if she'd never met Lily before, but she'd been a regular part of her life. All that knowledge did not help her to understand the child now. She'd changed; something had happened to her out there on the bridge—something more than just watching her mother killed. Something had shaken her to her very core, and Emily was bound and determined to find out what it was. If she couldn't, she wasn't sure Lily would ever be the same.

Emily stood outside Lily's door, but before she knocked, she could hear her inside the room.

"Red light—green light."

What does that mean?

She knocked, interrupting the child.

"Go away," Lily yelled.

"I ran bath water for you," Emily said as calmly as possible. "When you finish, your *vadder* expects you downstairs for breakfast."

There it was; she was putting the responsibility on Sam. It was the only leverage she had to use against the child. She didn't want to be too stern with her. She was suffering heartache and mourning the loss of her mother, but if she let the backtalk go on too long, it would become a regular habit, and that was not acceptable behavior.

Surely, the Bishop would put them under the ban if they could not get Lily's tantrums under control. Under normal circumstances, by Amish standards, she was too old to be acting

319

out in such a way, but she would discuss with Sam how long he would let it go on. The Bishop had warned him to get Lily under control or he'd have to put a temporary ban on them, which would prevent them from coming to church and participating in social functions until he could prove Lily's outbursts were restrained.

Emily went back downstairs to finish the breakfast since all she'd done was to put some fresh cinnamon rolls in the oven. She would leave Lily alone to bathe and dress while she cooked up some ham slices and scrambled some eggs.

Moments later, Lily entered the kitchen and plopped down at the table.

Emily turned from the stove and saw that she was still in her nightgown and hadn't even combed her hair.

"Go take a bath and get dressed for church, Lily," Emily said.

She shook her head.

Emily pointed upward. "Go, now; you will not be permitted to eat until you're ready for church."

Lily folded her arms over her chest and furrowed her brow.

"Lily, go upstairs and take a bath, or you'll miss breakfast and you'll have to go to church dirty and hungry—and in your nightgown."

"You're not my *mudder*," Lily said.

"Yes, she is, Lily," Sam said as he entered the kitchen from the back door.

Emily's heart jumped. She kept to herself and continued to crack eggs into a bowl, her back to Sam.

"She is your *mudder* now, and you will mind her. Go get your bath and be dressed and ready for the meal, and you better hurry or you'll go to church with an empty belly."

Lily let out a loud cry, continuing to sob as she went upstairs, stomping on each step along the way.

Emily turned to speak to Sam, but he'd disappeared from the room.

Her heart raced, and her breathing quickened. Tears rolled down her cheeks, and she wiped them away with the back of her hand.

Why had God put such a burden on her?

Chapter Twenty-Nine

The ride to the new Bishop's house was quiet; Sam had gone the long way around to avoid having to go on the bridge. She appreciated it, knowing it would likely upset Lily. She supposed it would probably hurt Sam too, but she suspected he did it more for Lily's sake than his own.

They arrived in plenty of time; several families arrived at the same time they did. Her heart thumped; there would be questions from members of the community—lots of questions. Questions she wasn't prepared to answer; should she have given potential questions a little more thought to keep from getting caught off guard?

It was too late to worry about it now. The Hochstetler family pulled up their buggy next to theirs. Linda had married Jeremy right after they'd turned eighteen and they had four young children already.

The men shook hands and Linda approached her. "I didn't know you were staying on," she said. "I thought you were only staying for a short visit."

"She's going to stay," Sam said, stepping in to save her from stumbling over an answer to an awkward question.

She supposed they would all be awkward for a while.

"Where are you staying? I'd love to visit with you," Linda asked.

"I'm staying at my house," she answered without thinking.

She hadn't meant to blurt it out, and judging by the drop of Linda's jaw and the bulging of her eyes, she was just as shocked as the Bishop had been when he was told.

"What will the Bishop say when he finds out?"

"We were married yesterday," Sam said, his voice cracking.

He said it a lot easier than she would have been able to.

Linda sucked in her breath, but quickly covered her mouth to cover her shock.

Emily watched Lily fidget and pull on Sam's arm to get his attention, but he ignored her. She was worried the child was going to make a scene over Sam's comment, and she was not prepared to handle any outbursts in front of everyone. She had no idea how other parents handled that from toddlers, but from an eight-year-old, it would be looked upon with disdain.

Thankfully, Sam continued to ignore her erratic behavior until it was time to go inside the house for the service.

They stepped inside the door and Sam peeled Lily off his arm. "You sit with Katie over there; you see her—she's with her *mamm.*"

Lily shook her head and frowned, whimpering quietly.

Emily's heart sped up.

Please, Gott, calm Lily's mind and help her to sit apart from her vadder.

Sam took her hand and tucked it into Emily's and then walked up toward the front of the room where the Bishop stood and said a few words to him. Then he sat on the right side with what seemed to be a few friends.

Lily stood next to her with her arms folded and a scowl on her face.

"Shall we sit?" she said to Lily.

The girl snatched her hand away and walked over to her friend, Katie. Little did she know that Emily knew her mother, Lydia. They'd gone to school together.

She followed Lily, and the girl flashed her a scowl and then sat with a harrumph next to Katie.

Lydia stood to greet Emily. "I see she's having a bit of rebellion toward you," she whispered.

Emily nodded and sighed.

"The best way to handle that is to ignore her and pretend you don't notice when she's acting that way; she's trying to get a reaction out of you, I think."

"Sam was ignoring her outside, and I suppose he already knows how to handle her, but I don't want to upset her."

Lydia shook her head. "That's the wrong attitude," she said. "The Bishop told us he married you two yesterday; I know it's hard filling Melody's shoes, but don't try. You do need to show her you're the parent—and her authority now. I know she's been through a traumatic thing, but she still needs discipline."

"I'm hoping she's going to accept me as time wears on," Emily said with a discouraging sigh.

Lydia smiled. "Trust me; the first time she needs you for something, she'll be over the attitude!"

"I pray you're right."

"We're neighbors, now," Lydia said. "We bought the old Bontrager place, so if you ever need anything, we aren't too far away. The girls meet between the properties and play almost every day. Jeremy made them a tree *haus* in the big oak tree; you can always find them there."

"That's *gut* to know if I'm ever looking for her." Emily smiled and sat next to Lydia to wait for the service to begin.

Chapter Thirty

Sam watched Emily from the other side of the Bishop's yard, where she and the other women were setting up food on the tables for the shared meal after church. It was such a lovely day; it was tough to grieve on such a day. The warm, Indian summer breeze clapping the already turning leaves together made him appreciate that he was alive. Melody loved the change of seasons, and the house was always filled with the aroma of pumpkin bread.

Would Emily make pumpkin bread?

He felt sorry for her; he knew she'd sacrificed a lot more than most women would. To take on the burden of an instant child and a husband in name only had to put a strain on her. He wouldn't know it by looking at her smile; it was as fresh as the morning dew.

It had been a long church service today, and with the awkward announcement of their impromptu marriage, she seemed to be holding up better than he was. He'd glanced back at her a few times and was happy to see Lily sitting quietly next to her. It was a relief to him that she didn't make a scene like she had at the funeral. Perhaps she would calm down after some time had passed, the way the doctor had advised him.

Now, as he watched Emily, he couldn't help but notice how truly beautiful she was. The breeze played with her blonde curls that had somehow escaped her prayer *kapp,* and her smile had not wavered. She seemed content to work alongside the women in the community, but she'd grown up with them, and it would be easy for her to fit back in.

He knew of the stories for the reasons behind her leaving the community; it was the reason he and Melody had rented her house. He worried some would pass rumors that he married her partly to stake a claim on her house, but it wasn't true. He'd only thought of his precious child without a mother. He'd spent many hours awake wondering if the decision he'd made was the right one, and he'd not given poor Emily much of a choice.

But watching her now as she cared for his daughter, he could only pray that in time he would be able to love her the way she deserved. She was a good woman, though he didn't know her very well, personally. Melody had always spoken very highly of her. Though it had not been an easy one, he was pleased with his decision to marry Emily.

Emily could feel Sam's eyes on her; it made her a little uncomfortable—as if she was being scrutinized. She prayed she was wrong, but she was embarrassed she wasn't able to control the child that was now hers. She wasn't certain what he expected from her, but she was feeling a little inadequate as a mother and a wife—both of which were nothing short of a big charade.

She'd put a letter in the mail to Eva, hoping to get some advice and even a visit. She knew it was a long trip with two little ones, but she needed her sister now more than anything. Lydia's offer had been kind, but it wasn't the same as having her sister to talk to about her troubles. She would likely be shocked at the marriage that was so soon it was almost scandalous. In her defense, it hadn't been her idea. She only prayed God would put love in her heart for the man, so she could one day be a wife to him if he'd have her as such.

The quiet ride home from the service seemed long; at least Lily was sleeping peacefully in the back seat of the open buggy. She'd worn herself out playing, and Emily had been happy to see her playing. She'd even caught her smiling once, but when their eyes met, the scowl returned. If Melody were here, she'd be able to tell her what to do, but she remained as quiet as possible in Sam's presence, not wanting to burden him further with her feelings of inadequacy at being an instant parent.

There was so much she'd wanted to ask Sam, but she felt awkward. Even now, sitting beside him in the buggy, their thighs bumped every time they hit a little bump in the road, and it caused her cheeks to heat with embarrassment.

Would it always be this way?

When they pulled into the yard, Sam halted the horse and hopped down to assist her out of the buggy. It was a sweet gesture, but it brought more heat to her cheeks. She turned away and cleared her throat when Sam hesitated before letting go of her waist. She wished her marriage could be under better circumstances, but God had put her in this one for a reason, and she would wait for Him to show her why.

Lily startled her by jumping out of the buggy and running toward the garden.

"You have chores to do, Lily, don't forget that," Sam hollered after her.

She waved a hand behind her without looking back, and Sam let out a heavy sigh.

Emily touched his arm lightly, the warmth of it sending prickles of heat all the way to her elbow.

"I know it's a small consolation," she said. "But she probably needs a break from behaving so well today."

He nodded and flashed her a half-smile.

"You're probably right; hold her accountable though," he urged her. "Make sure she feeds the chickens and gathers the afternoon eggs."

Emily forced a weak smile, thinking that it would be so much easier if she would just take care of the chore herself, but it was Lily's responsibility. "I will."

Chapter Thirty-One

Emily opened the door to find Katie standing there with a basket in her hands.

"Mamm sent these over to you; she thought you could probably use some help," she said matter-of-factly.

She took the basket and lifted the linen towel and was delighted and relieved to see two freshly-baked loaves of bread.

Was she that obviously inadequate as a parent and wife? She'd been there a couple of weeks already and hadn't been able to get caught up on anything. Dinner was always late, the wash was not being done all in one day, and she'd begun to get a little discouraged.

She took the basket over to the counter and bent to breathe in the aroma. She loved smelling freshly-baked bread when it filled the house, but she hadn't done much baking since she'd been back in her own kitchen.

Truth was, she'd gotten behind in her bread-baking and everything else since she'd taken on the full-time job of parenting and doing double chores. Lily had been slacking in hers, and she'd been picking up the slack for two reasons. She was hoping to give Lily a break and let her know she'd do anything for her, and she was trying not to look like a failure in Sam's eyes.

It didn't help matters that she'd been preoccupied with thoughts of wanting to be a real wife to Sam. They'd had plenty of awkward glances and accidental touches in the past few days, and she was beginning to wonder if a friendship might be blossoming between them. He'd become more talkative and inviting of companionship if nothing else.

Emily smiled at Katie. "Tell your *mamm danki* for me."

"I need the basket back so Lily and I can go pick blueberries."

Emily snapped away from the mesmerizing scent of the bread and focused on Katie. "Where are you picking blueberries?"

Katie pointed in the direction of the patch she knew well; it stood between her property and Bishop Byler's property.

Her heart sped up at the thought of the girls wandering that close to the unstable man.

Lily came bouncing into the kitchen, her hair in blond braids that hung just over her collarbones, her prayer *kapp* lopsided on her head. At least she was wearing it; Emily had bigger things to worry about, and let it go for the time being.

"Are you ready to pick blueberries?" Katie asked Lily.

The child smiled and nodded eagerly.

Emily sighed; this was going to hurt.

"I'm sorry," she said. "But you can't go, Lily, and I don't think you should go either, Katie."

Lily stamped her foot on the floor and folded her arms in front of her, the scowl Emily had begun to become familiar with forming on her face.

"Why?" she demanded.

"I don't want you venturing off too far from home."

It was a weak excuse, and judging by the child's growing anger in her eyes, she contemplated telling her the truth instead of giving her an excuse.

Truth was, Emily knew that patch of blueberries well. She and Eva used to pick the berries for their mother every summer. It was how they'd come to know Adam so well.

"We always go there," Katie said. "It's not too far."

It wasn't the distance that had her worried. Since the ladies at church had confirmed that the Bishop was indeed back on the property on house-arrest, she had no idea what his boundaries entailed; it was too much of a risk to think that he might not be able to wander around his own property, and that large patch of blueberries bordered both properties.

She had to assume they would allow him to work his land, and that would mean the girls might encounter him. She had no idea what he was capable of after he was arrested at Eva's house trying to see her *boppli*.

"Does your *mamm* know you were planning on going there to pick them?" Emily asked.

She shrugged. "She doesn't care."

"Well, I *do* care, and I'm asking you not to go over there anymore."

Lily stomped her foot again. "*Mamm* always let me go!"

"Well, that was before…" Emily stopped mid-sentence, not wanting to finish.

"I know," Lily said with a raised voice. "My *mamm*'s dead!"

That's not what she was going to say, but she could see how Lily might have taken it that way. She just didn't want them around the Bishop; if he wasn't home on house-arrest, it would be a different story. He wasn't stable and couldn't be trusted.

Lily began to cry. "I want some tarts—I want my *mudder.*"

"I'm sorry," Emily bent to hug Lily, but the child pushed her away and ran out the kitchen door.

She sighed and looked at Katie, who seemed spooked by the whole incident.

She turned to leave.

"Hold on a minute, Katie," she said as calmly as possible. "I'd like you to take your *mamm* a note for me, would you please?"

She nodded, but went over and stood by the door.

Emily quickly grabbed a pencil and a small pad of paper from the counter and wrote out a note explaining everything to her; surely, Lydia would agree with her reason for keeping the girls from that berry patch. At least she prayed it was so.

When she finished, she folded it up, praying the girl could not yet read cursive writing; she knew Lydia could because they'd attended school together.

"Take that to your *mudder* and ask her to send me back a reply," Emily instructed her.

She took the note and nodded, and then was out the door.

She picked up a male doll that she'd seen Lily working on the past couple of weeks and examined it. She'd fashioned his broadfall pants and made little suspenders, and added a white, yarn beard. When had she done that?

She wondered why she would make an older doll when most of the dolls that were still unfinished seemed to be young females, except for two that had brown beards. It struck her as odd, and something about it didn't feel right, but she couldn't put her finger on it. She brushed it aside, figuring Melody must have made a variety of dolls, even though she'd never seen any of them. The only ones she'd seen at the roadside stand had been sets of younger, *courting* couples.

She tossed it in the cedar chest along with the rest of the materials and went about finishing the basic cleanup. She'd left most of her family furniture in the house when she'd rented the house to Sam and Melody, so it was a little odd taking care of the home as the lady of the house.

She wished Lily would let her in her little world she was slowly closing herself up in, but the child hadn't spoken to her in more than a week. She'd been so angry about the note she'd sent to Lydia warning her to keep the girls away from the blueberry patch, she hadn't uttered even a word to her—not even to give her backtalk. It had been a quiet week, but at least when she was giving her backtalk, there was communication to build on.

The house had been silent, but she still wasn't doing her chores. She'd made one mess after another, and like now, with her sewing, Emily was picking up the slack and covering for her. She had a feeling Lydia would advise her not to do it, to let Lily get into trouble with her father, but Emily just didn't have the heart to do it. She could sense something was terribly wrong in Lily's world and she needed time to gain her trust; she truly thought that if she coddled Lily that she would eventually give in to her conscience and let Emily in.

Sam came in for lunch just as she was putting away the last of the things and closed the lid on the cedar chest. She turned around quickly at the noise, her hand flying up over her heart. He'd startled her.

He stood there for a minute, which made her nervous; had she done something wrong?

"How long are you going to keep doing Lily's chores?" he asked, suppressing a smile.

"I suppose that depends on how long you've known about it," she answered, teetering on her heels.

"I know you're trying to take it easy on Lily, but Melody was stricter than I am. You're not doing the child any favors—or yourself, for that matter, by trying to be her friend. She needs a *mudder*—she has Katie to be her friend."

Emily nodded, but it was tough for her to keep her concentration. She noticed his gaze travel to her lips a couple of times; did he want to kiss her? Adam had done that before he'd

347

kissed her for the first time. If he tried, did she want Sam to kiss her?

She did.

She'd been daydreaming too much about it—so much so, that she'd prayed almost day and night to keep her growing attraction toward Sam from burning her up with desire for him. She'd felt guilty for wanting a real marriage, but she would never make an advance toward him. If it was something he wanted, he would have to make the move.

"I believe in you, Emily," he said, gently. "You've been a *gut mamm* to her."

Her cheeks heated, and her gaze fell to the floor. "*Danki.*"

He closed the space between them and tucked his finger under her chin, lifting gently. Her heart sped up and her knees felt wobbly at his touch. His fingers explored her neck, sending shivers of excitement through her like falling embers from a lit sparkler when twirled on a warm summer night.

She extended her chin, exposing more of the flesh on her neck, allowing him to prod a little more. Her lips parted as he dipped his face toward hers, her breath held in.

His lips brushed gently against hers, causing her to moan slightly when she exhaled. Her hands went around his neck and her fingers raked through his hair, pulling him closer as she deepened the kiss.

A high-pitched scream from Lily rent the air, breaking the spell between them.

Emily broke her grasp on Sam and stepped back; breathless, she made eye-contact with Lily only long enough to see the tears welling up in her eyes. She took a step toward her, but Lily backed, turned around, and ran from the room, sobbing.

Emily started to go after her, but a firm hand on her arm stopped her. "Let her have some space; she's no more used to seeing us in an embrace than I am in being in the middle of it."

Oh no, did he regret kissing me?

"I think we're all going to need some time to get used to things," he said.

He bent and kissed her on the cheek and left the room; Emily collapsed onto the sofa after she heard the back door close, and wept quietly.

Chapter Thirty-Three

Lily finished pushing the sticks into the ground that outlined her makeshift bridge in the corner of her mother's garden. Then she placed the Bishop doll she'd sewn behind the sticks.

She wagged her finger at the doll. "You stay there where you can't hurt my *mudder!*"

Picking up her berry pail, she stood and watched the doll for a minute. "Don't you move!" she said to it.

351

After a few minutes, she broke her gaze on the doll and went off in the direction of the field to pick some blueberries for a make-believe tea party in the garden with her mother.

She headed out toward the field that separated their farm from the next one. She swung her tin, shallow pail by the handle as she walked through the meadow of alfalfa and clover that would soon be ready for the next cutting and baling. The thin, green blades swayed in the breeze, tickling her as she walked through it; in some spots, it was as tall as she was.

Her father had let the mowing go for longer than he should have for the final baling, but come winter, it would be in the barns of most of the community. Even she knew some of that money would fund a meager Christmas for her; that meant sugary confections in her stocking that would hang from the fireplace, perhaps a store-bought book to read, or a new pair of ice skates since she'd outgrown her other pair.

She put away the whimsical thoughts of the upcoming season and worried about gathering the last of the berries before the first frost would take them.

When she reached the berry patch, she filled her pail quickly, but decided to indulge in a few before she left the patch of overgrown bushes. She set her pail down on the ground, so she could grab them with both hands. They were so tasty, and she'd missed the afternoon meal because she was hiding.

The snap of a twig pricked her ears at the same time a shadow loomed over her. Her gaze lifted from the blueberry bushes; the sun was behind him and cast a shadow over his angry face, but she knew him.

The berries in her hands dropped slowly to the ground and she swallowed hard the mouthful she'd been chewing on, nearly choking on it. Her gaze fell to her pail on the ground at her feet, but her focus was on the green light that turned red when he took a step toward her.

Red light—green light.

"I remember you," he said with a crooked, half-smile. "I told you we'd meet again."

He was the man from the bridge.

She eyed her pail of berries; could she snatch the pail without him grabbing for her? She knew he couldn't reach her without the mechanical device on his ankle turning red; did it hurt him when it was red?

Although he couldn't go any further in the field, the pail was between them, and he could reach the pail.

"I warned you, didn't I?" he asked, grabbing for her arm. He caught her wrist and he teetered over the edge, his alarm blinking red and beeping.

Lily squealed; she fought him, twisting her arm, but he was too strong. He scooped her up by her waist and hung her at his side, his other hand over her mouth to quiet her. She wriggled and cried, but he had her muzzled while he walked back toward his barn with her.

Emily searched all over the house for Lily, looking in the empty barn, and had even walked through the tall grass between the properties to look in the tree house. She wasn't anywhere to be found. She'd called for her at the edge of the deep flower garden, and she'd contemplated Lily was ignoring her; now she was certain of it.

There was simply nowhere else she could be. It dawned on her that Lily could be hiding from her because of what happened earlier between her and Sam, but if she didn't find her soon, she'd begin retracing her steps until she did.

When she reached the garden, she called for Lily, but she didn't answer. Panic filled her; was the child playing games with her, or possibly trying to get her into *trouble* with Sam? He'd gone into town for supplies, and it was the first time he'd left her alone with Lily, and she was failing at being a mother—miserably failing at it.

Tears welled up in her eyes, and a lump constricted her throat. Why would Lily run off if not to rebel even more? In the weeks that she'd been with them, the child had done nothing but rebel against her. She refused to do her chores, and so Emily had done them for her to make Sam think she had everything under control. She'd pretty much let the child run amuck, and it was wearing thin on her nerves. When he'd called her out for it and kissed her, she thought things were looking up—until Lily caught them off guard. Her tantrum and now her disappearance filled Emily with a feeling of dread.

She stood in front of the garden and called for her again, listening for any movement.

Nothing but silence, except for the rustling of the late summer leaves blowing in the cool breeze. The sun was sinking fast, and

Emily knew if she didn't find Lily soon, it would be too dark to look.

Gott, please help me find her. Be with her and give her wisdom and courage. Let her know I love her—as my own dochder.

Tears ran down her cheeks; it was the first time she realized she truly loved Lily—and Sam; she couldn't bear to lose his child any more than he could.

She had to find Lily—quickly.

Lily couldn't breathe around the hand that covered her mouth. Her stomach ached where his arm was wrapped around her like a sack of grain. Tears dripped from her eyes and mucous blew out of her nose in bubbles as she tried to breathe. She bounced around in his arms as he trudged across the uneven field; it was giving her a stomach ache and caused her to gag on the berries souring in her nervous stomach.

She tried to scream, but his hand clamped down on her face so hard it made her jaw ache. Fear of this man consumed her; she couldn't breathe.

She'd been so angry with her *vadder,* and determined to have her own way, that she hadn't even told Cousin Emily—her new *mamm,* where she was going.

No one would come looking for her.

"Let—me—go," she screamed around the fingers digging into her cheeks.

"I can't let you go; you saw what happened on the bridge," he said.

Tears ran down her face. "I won't—tell—anyone," she cried around his strong hand covering her mouth.

"I'm going to bury you behind the barn, so you can be with your *mudder.*"

Lily's heart raced, and her blood ran cold; her eyes rolled back as she gave up her fight, and everything went black.

Chapter Thirty-Four

Emily ventured into the garden, calling out for Lily. Something at the far corner caught her eye, and she stepped cautiously toward it, unsure of what to make of it.

Behind a row of sticks poking into the dirt, was the old Amish doll with the white beard. Her heart flip-flopped when she noticed the black hat and coat. Only one man dressed like that in the community; Bishop Byler.

Had she seen him since he'd been out of jail?

Emily picked up the doll, her blood running cold when she noticed the band around the doll's ankle. She moved it closer to get a better look at it; Lily had used her crayons to draw a red and green dot on the band.

Red light—green light!

Oh no! Gott, please, no!

A high-pitched scream raised the hair on the back of Emily's neck.

The frightening pitch and volume let her know Lily was not far off; it sounded as if it came from the direction of the old Bishop's house.

Lily groaned; her lashes fluttered, but she couldn't seem to muster up the energy to open her eyes. Metal hitting hard-packed soil and rocks formed a constant rhythm in her head. Was someone digging?

She pulled in a breath, but something bound her mouth. She tried to move, but her wrists were tightly bound. At her back was a hard surface; she felt with her fingers. It was barn wood, but whose barn?

Lily forced her eyes open; a few feet away from her, the old man from the bridge was busy digging a large hole.

Emily ran toward the field that separated the two properties, her breath hitching and tears spilling from her eyes; she had no idea what the old man was capable of, but if his son was any indication, Lily was in danger!

Emily spotted the Bishop with Lily; she was struggling in his arms, a gag in her mouth and her hands were bound with twine. Her breath hitched, and she bit back tears, wondering how she was going to help her child.

Lord, help me save her!

Emily froze, fear overwhelming her as she watched him carry Lily over to what looked like a freshly-dug grave; the shovel was spade-down in a mound of dirt to the other side of the large hole. That shovel was between them. If he was distracted enough, she could try for it. The spade would make a threatening weapon.

She peered around the corner of the barn, her eyes darting between Lily, who was screaming and kicking, to the shovel she needed to save her.

A twig snapped under her foot and caused the Bishop to whip his head around toward her.

"Who are you?" he barked at her through gritted teeth.

"I am her *mudder!*"

He chuckled. *"Nee,* I remember you! You're Eva's *schweschder;* I made sure that horse tossed her off the bridge, and now you're next," he said, glancing back and forth between her and Lily.

"Eva didn't…" Emily stopped midsentence when she noticed the look of horror on Lily's face. He *had* been there that day, and it was somehow his fault Melody was dead. He'd obviously mistaken her for Eva since they look so much alike.

She gulped; that could have been her if she and Eva were identical twins!

"After I take care of this little witness, I'll take care of you too. I'm not giving you the chance to put me back in jail!"

Lily wriggled in the Bishop's arms. "Help me, *Mamm,*" she cried.

It was the first time she'd recognized Emily as her mother; she would save her daughter, or she would die trying.

"Let her go!" Emily demanded.

She dove for the shovel and grabbed it, rolling onto her side and scrambling to her feet before he could grab her. She raised the shovel over her shoulder. "Don't make me hit you, old man!"

He dropped Lily into the shallow grave and dove for Emily. Lily hit the ground with a groan and then began to cry.

"Help me!" she screamed.

The Bishop tackled Emily and he pinned her down with one arm and raised the shovel above his head with the other.

"Drop it!" a male voice said from behind her. "Drop the shovel and put your hands high where I can see them."

Bishop Byler lowered the shovel slowly, his focus on whoever was facing him. He rose from the ground, and that's when Emily noticed his ankle bracelet blinking nonstop red. She turned around and scooted back toward the officer. They must have come because of the signal.

Lily poked her head up from the shallow grave he'd dug to bury her in; it sent shivers down Emily's spine. She scrambled to her feet as the officers put the Bishop in handcuffs.

She went to Lily and scooped her up into her arms and held her close, allowing her to sob freely.

"It's all over, honey," she said, soothing her daughter. "You're safe now; I'm not going to let anyone hurt you. I love you, Lily."

She laid her head on Emily's shoulder and sniffled. "I love you too, *Mamm.*"

Emily bit back tears of joy; her little girl was safe.

One of the officers approached her. "Are either of you hurt?" he asked.

Emily shook her head. "Just a little scared."

He put a hand on Lily's back and patted her. "There's no reason to be afraid anymore; he'll be going back to jail for a long time."

"How did you know we were here?" she asked.

"We didn't; his alarm tripped several times and then it stayed on because he was out of his zone too long, so we came out here to see why, and that's when we saw him trying to hurt you. Is that a grave he dug?"

Lily lifted her head from Emily's shoulder. "*Jah*, he said he was going to bury me!" she cried. "He's the man who killed my *mudder!*"

Emily fought tears, thinking how close she came to losing Lily.

The officer took their names and address, and then informed them they would be contacted to give a formal statement.

"Would you like a ride home?" the officer asked.

She shook her head. "No, we have something to get, so we'll go back through the field; it isn't far."

"I think I'd feel better if one of us escorted you home," he said.

She nodded; maybe it would be best.

"If we go through the field, it only takes five minutes, but if you go out on the road, it will take longer," she said.

He held a hand out toward the open field. "Lead the way."

Emily and Lily wandered back through the field, hand-in-hand, Emily feeling relieved they were out of danger, and thankful that the police had gotten there in time. But most of all, she felt blessed that Lily had finally accepted her as her mother.

When they came upon the blueberry patch, Emily spotted Lily's full bucket of berries still sitting on the ground and bent to pick it up.

"Let's go home and make some blueberry tarts for your *vadder*, shall we?" she asked.

Lily looked up at her and smiled. "Okay, *Mamm*.

Chapter Thirty-Five

Emily sat across from Lily at the little table inside the entrance to the garden, sipping meadow tea and nibbling on blueberry tarts.

Lily had talked non-stop about how excited she was for school to begin the following week, but Emily savored every little giggle from her. Sam walked by and smiled at them as he walked the team of draft horses out of the barn so he could bring them to the field to finish the hay-mowing. She watched her husband for a moment, thinking how lucky she was that a man such as Sam loved her.

He'd moved his things back into the main house, and he'd asked her to join him, leaving her childhood bedroom behind. He'd commented the empty room would make a nice place to put Lily's old crib for a new *boppli*, and she'd giggled shyly.

"*Dat*, come sit with us and share our blueberry tarts," Lily begged.

He smiled and tied the horses to the large oak tree in the yard.

"I'd much rather sit and have tea and tarts with *mei familye,*" he said with a chuckle as he sat down between them. "The hay-mowing can wait another day!"

THE END

Made in the USA
Middletown, DE
13 April 2019